I0734815

OUTPOURING

BOOK SIX of *THE STARLIGHT CHRONICLES*

C. S. Johnson

For Sam. Every word I have written, I have written that you might believe, both in God and in the love and truth that sets both of us free.

I would also like to dedicate this book to my special fans in my favorite Mrs. Wong-Johnson's class, Kekoa and Marley. We are on separate halves of the world, and it is all wonder to me that my words can inspire you. Every artist has days of crippling insecurity, but thanks to you and your kindness and your enthusiasm, I have a perpetual silver lining in the clouds of doubt.

To Get *Awakening* (A Special Christmas Episode of The *Starlight Chronicles*) as a bonus for picking up this book,

Download It At:

https://www.csjohnson.me/awakening

Check out *Reflecting* (A Dream Episode of The *Starlight Chronicles*), a short story that takes place before Book 5.

THE STARLIGHT CHRONICLES

5

THE STARLIGHT CHRONICLES

6

☼1☼
Warmth and Wakefulness

It was not the usual matter of desperation that fueled me forward, as I ran in the rain, heading toward my favorite coffee shop.

Don't get me wrong; despite the early, early morning hours, I fully expected to be greeted with a steaming, warm cup of coffee, one that was perfect for warding off the chill in the air. I knew I was going to need it to get through the day, and it was likely I was going to need the second or third cup I would leave with, too. But in recent months, coffee had become the secondary reason that I loved to stop in and sit for a while at Rachel's Café. (It was not a love easily dethroned, either.)

Coffee had been my true love, until I'd found my *true* true love.

I glanced up to see the soft light coming from the room on the second floor. *She's awake.*

I pushed open the back door to the small café and headed up the stairs, as silently as possible, and then all of a sudden there I was, standing in the doorway to her room. The echo of the rain was slightly louder, as the newly renovated wall in her room still needed some work, but the soft glow of her desk lamp was on, casting a small shadow of relief against the thunderstorm outside.

"Raiya."

She was sitting on her bed, her eyes glowing with wakefulness as she remained curled up in the warmth of her covers.

"What are you doing here, Hamilton?" she asked, her voice bracing against the subtlety of the night. There was no accusation in her tone, just surprise.

"I wanted to check in on you," I admitted, suddenly feeling dumb.

"At five-thirty in the morning?" Raiya asked. "I know I told you I've been having trouble sleeping, but it's—"

"Sorry." I scratched my head, suddenly very aware of how wet and cold I was. "I had a dream about you. I wanted to make sure you were okay."

"So you ran all the way here?" Raiya's lips curled into thoughtful smile. "You didn't want to call me?"

I considered arguing with her, which I would have delighted in, but thought the better of it. She was more beloved to me than arguing, too. "No."

"No?"

"I wanted to see you."

She pushed back her covers, allowing me a good grin at her fluffy-pants pajamas, and came over to me. "I'm glad you're here," she admitted, "and I would hug you, but you're all wet. Come on. I'll get you a towel and a cup of coffee."

"I feel like a king already," I said, although I probably looked more the part of the pauper. Even moments later, as my hands wrapped themselves tightly around my mug and a towel was draped over my shoulders, I felt more of the part of the humble and helpless, while I'd meant to be the hero.

"How's that?" she asked. "I can't imagine you're warmed up yet, but hopefully it'll help."

"You're the only *Raiya sunshine* I need," I assured her.

As she rolled her eyes and walked past me with a handful of creamers, I tugged on her shirt, pulling her in close. "Thank you," I said, as I finally got to kiss her again.

Raiya chuckled as she drew back. "It's my pleasure."

"No, *you're* my pleasure," I replied, staring at her long enough to make her blush.

She redirected me immediately; for all the brashness and boldness she had to stand up to me and my opinions, I knew and appreciated that Raiya had a modest side.

"Tell me about the dream you had. It must've been pretty bad if you're coming here this late," she prompted, as she moved to the other side of the counter. I knew she was making some tea. She loved her espresso as much as I did, but she was more of a tea drinker in the mornings, and I loved her for it. "Or should I say this early, since Rachel won't be here for another two hours?"

"Letty won't wake up, will she?" I asked, suddenly dreading the thought of Rachel's old-lady mother coming cranking down the stairs as we spent our time together.

"Not likely," Raiya said, effectively putting my shallow fears to rest. "I've been taking the morning shifts here at the café, since I dropped out of school. Aunt Letty doesn't usually wake up till noon anymore. Unless, of course, she hears me when I wake up in the middle of the night. But the rain should provide some cover tonight."

"I can't tell you how lucky you are, getting to drop out," I said. "Even if AP Gov is not the same without you to argue with."

"I imagine it's much more peaceful," she said neutrally.

"Peace might seem like an attractive offer," I said, "but I'll take arguing with you over semantics and historicity and context any day of the week."

"How is Mrs. Smithe?" Raiya asked. "Has she said anything else to you about SWORD lately?"

"Not since January," I said. "Almost two months later, and nothing in all that time."

"She's not the only one who's gone quiet," Raiya said as she sat down across from me. Her eyes fell to the seat that her grandfather, the esoteric and elusive Grandpa Odd, would sit in, and my reasons for scurrying over to see her immediately jumped to the forefront of my mind.

I reached out for her hand. "Everything will be alright," I said.

She squeezed my hand in return. "I'm not sure *you* know that," she replied easily enough. She sipped from her own mug with a peace I envied.

Raiya had a point, as she usually did, and it was a big one. If I truly believed things would be okay, why did I come running to see her before daybreak?

I shoved that thought aside. I loved her. I wanted to be with her. I knew we faced a considerable challenge. So, there was nothing inherently wrong with running through the rain and the dark of the night to see her.

"I'll admit, I'd feel better if we knew where Draco was hiding," I said bitterly. "I guess it didn't matter if he had his dragon skin or not. He's still terrible to try to locate."

"Agreed."

"He hasn't been here, has he?" I asked.

"No," Raiya said, shaking her head. I watched, transfixed, as some of her gingerbread hair broke free from the loosened bun at the back of her head. "Rachel and Aunt Letty were surprised to hear he went missing after the last attack near Rosemont. They haven't made much of a thorough investigation, but that's more because of the 'police' jurisdiction than anything else."

I snorted. "SWORD's going to have to think of a better cover soon."

"They've gotten away with sillier explanations," Raiya pointed out. "They've done more clean-up around the city, as far as damage goes. That's probably the reason that the assistant mayor's willing to let it slide for now."

I shrugged. "Assistant Mayor Dunbrooke doesn't seem as interested in the supernatural stuff as Stefano did."

"That's probably because he hasn't been taken over by a Sinister or a demon monster," Raiya replied.

"So far as we know." I frowned, thinking of the small, wiry man who seemed more machine than man, especially when it came to running what he referred to as "his domain." Which included me, for the three or four days a week I would go into work at City Hall.

I didn't mind that much. At least he was smart enough to leave me alone.

"True." Raiya smiled. "You have me there."

"Did I tell you that he's ordered the judiciary council to give Cheryl a deadline to produce the city superheroes?" I asked. "She has ten days to find them or the case is getting dismissed. Dunbrooke says it's costing the city time, money, and manpower."

"I'll bet your mom didn't like that."

"No," I said. "She didn't, putting it mildly. Blowing up ballistically when she got the report is more accurate."

Raiya laughed. "I would've loved to see her face. It's not often that the famous Cheryl Thomas-Dinger, the Queen of Apollo City Courtrooms, doesn't get her way."

"I'll try to get a picture of it when her time's up and she's left without us to fight in court."

"I'm assuming that your dad hasn't told her the truth about us?"

Thinking of my dad made me flinch. I shook my head. "No. He wouldn't. He knows how to keep secrets. And he's mandated to do so, with healthcare laws as they are. Or so he says. I can see him working around them if he wanted. Or," I added, "if Chery wanted."

When Raiya's grandfather revealed himself to be not only Elysian's rebellious brother Draco but also the mysterious Ogden Skarmastad, the founder of Apollo City, he gave us quite a surprise. And an unwelcome one, at that.

But finding out my father had known about SWORD and my secret superhero identity smashed through me. Since then, it was as if a chasm of secrets had suddenly pushed itself between us, damaging the ideas we had about each other irrevocably.

Mark usually came home late, left for work early—which really wasn't out of the norm—and our interaction was limited to the raw food dinners my mother's latest chef, a sushi master named Ayako, was making for us. We didn't talk much.

Raiya nodded. "I guess if he didn't tell her about me, he wasn't going to tell her about you. He loves you very much."

"Psh." I finished my coffee. "Coffee and intellectual levels, that's really all we have in common. And even with that, I'm pretty sure I'm smarter, and he likes his coffee darker."

"You really think you're smarter than your father?" Raiya arched her brow at me.

"I'm not the one who's best friends with a SWORD operative," I reminded her.

"Good point. You're making a lot of good points, despite being up this early," she observed.

"I know you're trying to get me off the original argument because you can't win," I told her, "but I'll humor you because I love you."

"I know you're just charming me because you're afraid I will come up with something better," Raiya responded. "But I'll humor you, because I love you, too."

I grinned. "Intellectual banter is so much fun with you."

"It always was for me," Raiya said. "Although I do miss you getting ticked off with me for winning before you knew who I was. That was pretty amusing."

"Ha, ha." I laughed drily. "If it makes you feel better, I'll start getting more angry when you attempt to win. But anyway, there are good reasons I'm awake and I'm here."

"Yes, you should tell me those." Raiya sipped her tea thoughtfully. "You mentioned the dream. Is there something else? Is Elysian bothering you?"

"I wish," I admitted. "He's been pretty alert and disciplined since Draco's reappearance. He probably sleeps less than you do."

"A considerable feat," Raiya said with a laugh. "Although I probably sleep more than you realize. I take naps after Letty relieves me, before you're out of school and swim practice."

"Thankfully the season's over now." I shook my head. "No new records this year, but still a lot of wins."

"Maybe you'll break some records next year," Raiya said.

"Will we be done with this mission by then?" I asked. *That would be super. Absolutely perfect, actually. The sooner this is over, the happier I will be.*

She shrugged. "I don't know. But there's no harm in hoping."

"I'm just hoping that I'll stop having these premonitions in the middle of the night." I sighed. "As much as I love you, and I love seeing you, Mark's already not exactly happy with me, and Cheryl's passive-aggressive enough to make me worried. I don't want to be punished for feeling like I need to come to your rescue."

"Couldn't have been that bad, even if you did run all the way here, and in the rain, no less."

"It was bad enough." I tapped my empty cup on the counter. "In my dream, I just saw you looking sad, like you were upset, so I wanted to come and rescue you."

Raiya pursed her lips. "I know that when I was in the hospital and attacked, you were scared," she said carefully, "but there's no reason to believe I was in immediate danger."

"Attacked" was the tidy way to summarize Raiya getting her heart smashed and her soul ripped out of her body just weeks ago. I clenched my fingers together, trying not to shout at her for her flippancy.

I calmed down enough before replying with, "I know."

I know, but I couldn't help it. Maybe I wanted to come more for me, than you.

"Are you sure you weren't the one who wanted me to comfort you?"

Hearing my own thoughts echoed back to me just made me more frustrated. "No," I insisted.

Raiya was smarter than that. "I know you better than you realize, you know." She laughed. "I still remember that whole issue last year with your birthday cake."

"I can't believe I apologized to you for that. I take it back."

She smirked. "It's too late, I already took it."

I stuck my tongue out at her, before sinking into silence.

"I know it doesn't help you any with Mikey still in the hospital," she added, after a while.

I still said nothing. Mikey had been my best friend, like my brother at one point. Now, he might as well have be permanently planted in the hospital bed where we could occasionally go to visit. As swim season dwindled down, I had a harder time not telling him he was going to pay for just lying around all day and night. At least the poor quality hospital food was keeping him from getting fat.

His mind and heart had seemed to heal more. He was, apparently, doing better with the tutor Central had sent over, and he seemed more like his old self when we went to see him.

Sometimes.

Then Mikey would remember he was supposed to hate me and I'd been the one who'd caused the demise of his true love, or whatever he wanted to call her, who just happened to be my ex-girlfriend.

I didn't think it was my direct fault that Gwen got her Soulfire stolen by Taygetay, one of the last of the Seven Deadly Sinisters we'd captured. If I had to make a case for it in court, I could probably make it convincing. But sometimes, when I did present the case inside my mind, it went back and forth enough between the "innocent" and the "guilty" verdict. It made me uncomfortable.

The best thing I could do, as far I as could figure—and Raiya agreed with me on it—was work to free Gwen's Soulfire.

It was probably going to take some time to destroy Draco, and *that* was of no comfort to Mikey, especially since he'd witnessed Gwen's pain.

I still had trouble seeing his PTSD diagnosis, but I did know that part of the reason for it was true, and the other reason was for his protection.

His estranged father, Dante, my less-than-agreeable and less-than-amicable, most-of-the-time contact from SWORD, was keeping him there. And I could appreciate it, because he was keeping him from my mother interrogating him about the identities of Wingdinger and Starry Knight—me and Raiya, respectably.

"Maybe he'll get out once the timeline on the case is over," I said. "Stefano said before only Cheryl could get to him now. Maybe once she's out of the way, the statute of limitations will be over, and Dante will allow Mark to give him a clear discharge."

"Maybe." It was Raiya's turn to shrug. She glanced outside the windows, where the rain was picking up, pitter-pattering down as it washed the world clean.

She picked up my empty cup and poured me a new one. "Let's not worry about it now."

"What?" Incredulously, I looked at her as if she'd gone crazy. "How can we *not* worry about this?"

"Talk to me about other things," she said. "Tell me stories of all the other girls at school terrifying you, thinking that

THE STARLIGHT CHRONICLES

you're not secretly in love with your coffee barista. Tell me about the swim team drama this semester."

When my mouth just dropped open, appalled at her appeal to the meaningless, she smiled. "I can tell you about some of the daytime soaps that Aunt Letty leaves on upstairs, if you can't think of something more interesting."

"Don't we have to worry about this?"

"We've worried about it for a long time," she said. "I need a break. Just a small one." She came around and sat down next to me.

Tentatively, I nodded. "Okay. I can think of more interesting things than Letty's soap operas. If you're sure you want to."

"I do," she said. "We'll go crazy trying to figure out everything right now. Let's just be normal for a bit."

"I can't argue with that," I said, and then I obliged her with stories of Poncey's latest pranks, the swim team's gluten-free swim-ghetti disaster, and Via's constant attempts to push her new boyfriend in my face, despite my eternal apathy.

I watched in wonder as she made faces and comments and more coffee.

It was a good two hours I got to spend with her, on a cold, rainy, late March morning, with nothing else to look forward to, except coming back to her at the end of the day. As Rachel came in, and customers soon after her, I wondered if I would have a "normal" life like that, where I wouldn't have to

say good-bye to the "normal" parts and slink back to into the
dread that accentuated my day.

☼2☼
Ordinary

To be fair, most of my day was still "normal." It just wasn't any real fun.

To be *really* fair, I don't suppose eleventh grade was really supposed to be fun. There's good reason the proverbial "they" have a special category for "angst" when it comes to teenagers.

"What do you think, Dinger?"

I glanced up from my computer screen to see Evan, better known as Poncey to me and my friends, looking at me expectantly. "What do I think about what?"

"Come on, man, were you listening at all?" Poncey sighed. "I was just telling you that Jason totally failed at asking Laura Nelson to the prom."

"Prom?"

"Uh, yeah, that huge party that we're all going to next month, remember?" Poncey reached over and poked my forehead.

I frowned at him before turning back to my work.

"It's that party you said you would even cancel your birthday party for since it's the same weekend."

It was very clear, at this point, I knew what he was talking about. I didn't know if he was doing this shtick to get me angry or not. It seemed that of late, my friends had been more determined than ever to get on my bad side.

"I get it, Poncey," I snapped. "I'm just trying to work. Give me a break."

"Calm down, dude. Anyway, Laura was flirting with him like she was just hoping that he would ask, and he did—"

"Yeah, that's nice," I grumbled.

"Hey, Mr. Gallows is out talking to the principal. You don't have to worry about getting in trouble." Poncey gestured toward the front of the computer lab, where I could clearly see Poncey was right. "Besides, it's Mr. G. He wouldn't punish us at all. He's too nice."

"Uh-huh," I muttered. "I'm working on my project."

Poncey shuffled himself in front of my screen. "No you're not. You're reading the local news!"

"You say it like it's a bad thing," I replied. "And I need some info for my project. That graphics project's not going to make itself."

"What do you need to know about"—Poncey peered closely at my screen—"the Flying Angels case?"

"I was looking for a picture," I lied.

"Well, you're going to get an A anyway. I don't know why you worry about it."

"Because I actually have to do the work to get the A," I answered. I was tempted to remind him of all the times I'd been the one who did his work so he could get an A, too, but I decided against it. I had more important things to worry about.

Such as the *Flying Angels v. Apollo City* case. The D. A., my mother, had filed for an extension. The courts would decide in a few days if she could have more time to produce the suspects in question. Other than that, they didn't give much information. Not that there would be a whole lot. Still, I nearly laughed at it. The media was clearly trying to appease the new mayor, since they'd taken out a lot of their commentary (they hadn't held back any chances to blister about Wingdinger and Starry Knight before, when Stefano was sane and still in good health.)

"So who are you taking to prom?" Poncey asked.

"Um … what?" I turned back to face him after skimming through the rest of the article. "Oh, prom. I don't know. I might not take anyone."

"Come on, Drew's taking Simon's younger sister, Phoebe, and I'm going to take Felicia," he said. "Jason's been shot down, and Mikey's not likely to come, being hospitalized and all—"

"I don't know who I'm going to take," I said blandly. "I'll worry about it later."

Poncey frowned. "What's wrong with you, man?"

"What do you mean?"

23

"You're just acting weird lately," Poncey said. "I mean, you don't seem that interested in what's going on with all of us. Drew and Jason, and me, and all of us—we're your friends."

"Hey, I come to your parties," I objected. "I was just at Jason's last week, when he had that video game party all-nighter."

"And you sat there and just played and commented about half as much as usual." Poncey leaned back in his chair. "It just seems like you're not really paying attention to us anymore. Don't you care?"

"Of course I care," I snapped. "But I have a lot to do."

"You can tell us that," Poncey said. "We won't get upset with you for being busy, man."

"Well, I'm busy right now. I'm not going to worry about getting a prom date. Especially since it's a whole month away."

"All the good girls will be gone," Poncey warned me.

"I'll survive," I assured him. "But first," I said, trying to soften my tone some so it didn't seem like I was being so defensive, "I have a few things to take care of."

"That's right," Poncey declared, the rush of remembering in his voice making me instantly suspicious, "we have the SATs coming up."

I nearly groaned before I realized that was the perfect excuse for my moodiness. "Duh!" I said. "Why else would I be so on edge lately?"

"Yeah, I can't blame you. I signed up for that SAT class and I'm just totally *freaking* out," Poncey said. He continued talking to me about this while Mr. Gallows came back into the class.

When Mr. Gallows glanced my way, I gave him a rueful smile and shrugged. Mr. G was a good guy. He was one of those teachers that didn't ask for much; he didn't expect you to change the world with his imparted knowledge. He just helped you out as much as you wanted, and then let you be on your way.

He's still one of my all-time favorite teachers.

Mr. Gallows seemed to get my message that Poncey was hopeless, and there was no point in trying to get him to stop talking.

After class ended, and Poncey was still talking to me, I almost wish I'd advocated harder for Mr. Gallows to come and stop him.

"Drew and I are rounding up some people to get another season of Ultimate Frisbee up again," Poncey said. "You want to play with us more this time?"

"Well, I do love Ultimate," I agreed. "I'll pencil it in. Text me when you've gotten a time locked down."

"Sure thing, Dinger," Poncey said with a grin. "We're going to meet up next week after school, in Shoreside Park."

"Oh, cool." It was on the way to Rachel's at least. It was possible I would be able to stop by when I went to go see Raiya after school.

"Hey, Poncey, Dinger, wait up!" Jason, another one of my best friends, skipped up from behind us. "Can't believe it's not the weekend yet."

"I know, really." Poncey shook his head. "Not that this one counts for most of us, right?"

"Huh?" Jason looked confused.

"SATs, man. Where've you been?"

Poncey joined Jason in arguing over plans for the week, while I slipped out of the conversation.

The Flying Angels case's extension would be decided soon. If it was denied, I would be free of Cheryl's likely torture in court as of next week, even if I had to put up with her resulting tyrannical outbursts at home.

I prayed that it would be alright in the end. I was getting tired of that particular threat. Wanting to be a lawyer and getting caught up in the very system you want to learn how to manipulate didn't sit well inside of me.

A sudden movement caught my attention; I saw a sliver of light flashing off a coffee thermos. It was Martha.

A sudden impulse struck me, and I was unwilling to let it go.

"Hey guys, I'll see you later," I said, waving while I was already sliding away. "Gotta talk to Martha.

Martha—or Mrs. Smithe, until I graduated (got to be proper about these things, you know)—had admitted to me she knew about SWORD, and she'd used to work for them. I knew that she knew about other things, too, not the least of which was that I was Wingdinger and Raiya was Starry Knight, and that we were dating.

Maybe, I thought, *maybe I can get her to help me. We need something to go on, after all.*

Raiya and I were not going to succeed just waiting around for Draco to come crawling out of his hiding spot and announce himself. He'd been hiding out as Raiya's half-ancient grandfather for decades. Who knew how long it would take him to show his creepy, scaly, demonic dragon face around Apollo City again?

If anyone *would* know, it would be SWORD.

Maybe Martha was my ticket to finding SWORD.

"Mrs. Smithe," I said, as I inserted myself into her path. "I've been looking for you."

"What is it?" she asked, stepping around me and indicating that I should follow. "Speak quickly, because I have another class in three minutes."

"I was wondering if I could talk to you in private?"

"No." Her dark eyes were hard as steel as she looked at me. "I told you, I have a class in three minutes."

I sighed. "It's about SWORD," I said softly.

I should've known better than to ask her about that and expect her to be surprised. She narrowed her gaze even further, but her voice dropped its volume as she spoke.

"I've been expecting you to ask me questions for a while," she said. "It's about time. I would not have expected this long of a wait from you, Dinger."

I blushed, flustered. "I've been … "

"Distracted, bored, or busy?" she asked. "It's always one or the other with you lately. I can't believe Raiya dropping out of school has affected you this much."

"It's not just that," I told her. "We've been … " My voice trailed off as I realized we hadn't been doing that much. We discussed things, Elysian and I took turns at patrol, and Raiya kept an eye and an ear out for any whispers from where we knew we could get answers. But we were at a dead end. "Okay, we've run out of options."

"Waiting is generally the safe option," Mrs. Smithe said, not in agreement, but more out of default. "What it is you want to know?"

"Can we talk about this later?" I asked. "We both have class."

She stopped by her door, and then swiveled around. While she was shorter than me by a good deal, her gaze was sharp enough to make me straighten up. "Listen to me," she said, "and listen well, Hamilton. SWORD has a lot of resources, and they know of my position here. It's better if you don't actively seek my company quite so much, or they'll suspect you."

"They probably already do," I argued.

"That doesn't mean I want to make it worse." Martha huffed. "Now, we have a minute before class begins again. Ask your questions."

"I need to find SWORD," I said. "They've been hired by the city under the name Otherworld, Inc., but the Skarmastad Foundation is footing the bill. While I know where one of the agents is, I can't always go to him, either."

"You want to know where the business is?"

"Sort of. I'm not sure what kind of information would help."

"Those are poor research skills right there, Dinger."

"I know." I shrugged. "I'll fix it before college."

"Ha! That's a riot. But for SWORD, there's no reason I would know where they are now," she said. "I've been decommissioned, and for over a decade now."

"Do you know anything that would help us?" I asked.

"I don't know where their base is now, but I can probably find out," she said slowly. "But I need you to tell me something."

"Anything," I agreed.

"What is your goal with all of this?"

I looked at her, dumbfounded. "What do you mean?" I asked. I felt like I'd been asking that question a lot since I'd found out about my superpowers.

"I mean, what are you doing? I've seen what you and your friends do."

"We protect people."

"But what else?"

"What else?" I echoed the question like it was in a foreign language.

"Yes, what else?"

"What else do we need to do?" I asked, my tone now exasperated. "We do plenty."

"You're on the defensive. It's a losing position." Mrs. Smithe shook her head. "You need to start going on the offensive."

I suddenly understood what she was saying. "You're right," I admitted. "We don't have much of a game plan. We don't have a long-term plan, either."

"Tell you what," Mrs. Smithe said. "If I can get you the location of SWORD and its branches, then you have to do something for me."

I sincerely hoped it had nothing to do with AP Government or Mock Trial. She was already mad at me for not signing up this year. But I nodded. "Okay. What is it?"

"You should never promise something that you don't know you can fulfill," Mrs. Smithe told me in her most serious voice. I balked at it, and I was wondering if that was what she wanted me to do when she said, "I want you to stop asking me about it after this. Like I said, they might suspect you. Or me."

"Then why did you tell me about working for SWORD in the first place?"

She ignored the question. "Come back to me in a few days, just like this, in between classes when the hallways are full, and I'll let you know what I've found for you."

"Thank you," I said. I smiled up at her, grateful. "Raiya says thank you, too."

"Oh, really?" Martha smirked. "And I guess your dragon does, too?"

"Oh, yeah, you know it," I replied with small laugh.

"Is he here to deliver that in person?" Martha gestured toward the window. I leaned over, peeking through the door of her class, and saw she was right. Climbing up the waterspout was my stubborn and belligerent changeling dragon.

"If he is," I said, "I'm going to intercept."

"Good idea," Mrs. Smithe agreed, before she brushed past me, and turned her attention to her blissfully unware and waiting class just as the bell rang.

Well, it looks like once more, I will be missing my last period class.

Who was I kidding? I didn't mind.

But I *did* mind Elysian sneaking around the school, and I was determined to remind him of that as I headed out to meet him.

It was getting easier to cut out of class, I noticed, as I walked through the hallways toward the locker rooms. There was an entrance I knew of from my swim team insider knowledge, and the upside to using it was that it was close enough I didn't have to circle back around much.

That alone was probably the reason I managed to sneak up behind Elysian without alerting him to my presence.

"I'm going to kill you for this one of these days," I said, picking him up by his lizard-neck.

"Ha!" Elysian looped his tail around my arm and clung to me; he knew that drove me crazy. "Sometimes you don't even see me, you know. I was wondering if I was going to have to go inside today or not."

"I doubt that," I said. "Considering how you've been sitting around my house watching the news while no one is there, I'm willing to bet that's just the story you're telling to make yourself look good."

"What other kind of story would *you* possibly know of?" Elysian huffed. "All your stories make you look good in the end."

"That's because I'm the hero," I asserted. "And because I have a natural talent for getting out of tough spots."

"I would only agree to that because everything that's natural dies."

"Just shut up," I grumbled, finally getting tired of our argument. "Tell me why you're here."

"Your girlfriend asked that I come and get you once you were finished," Elysian said.

"I'm not done with school yet! I have one more period to go."

He shrugged. "What does it matter to me?" he asked. "You're almost done, that's close enough in my book."

"Your book must be abridged for morons." I slapped him off my arm and tucked him up behind my backpack. "I'm already too late to get away with getting back in without being noticed. I might as well leave."

"See?" Elysian sneered. "You're already trying to make yourself out to be some hero for skipping school. Starry Knight's enjoying herself at the moment, talking with Logan at the Lakeview Observatory. She'll be fine while she waits."

I paused. Dare I admit it to Elysian?

"I'm worried about her," I said a moment later. "I had a dream about her the other night. She was alone and terrified and sad."

"She usually is."

"Hey!" I whacked him over the head. "She is not."

"She doesn't seem to have a lot of friends besides us," Elysian noted. "And a member of her own family ended up betraying her."

I thought about it, and then I remembered what I'd seen before, what I'd heard before. "Adonaias is waiting for her," I said. "Surely, between us and him, that's all she needs. Raiya's much more introverted than either of us."

Elysian shrugged. "I guess so."

"She has Rachel, too," I added, thinking of the pretty redhead who ran the café with her name on it. "And Letty."

"Letty's not what I would call ideal company," Elysian said.

"I would've thought you'd like her," I said with a grin. "She seems to smoke as much as you do."

"Ha, ha, ha," Elysian grumbled. "You're hilarious."

"She's got some claws, too, come to think of it," I added, starting to laugh at my own joke as we headed out of the school and toward the hill by the marina. Elysian snarled while I snapped, as we headed toward Lakeview Observatory.

☼<u>3</u>☼
Lakeview

Elysian eventually managed to ignore me properly as we walked through Shoreside Park and then along the pier, and I promptly returned the favor with fervor, thinking of possibly asking Raiya to take a walk by the water with me in a little while. It was still early, and the sun was still out, even if it was chilly. We would have the time, and I wanted it.

Ever since she'd come back from visiting Alora, the Star of Time, and found out the truth of Grandpa Odd, Raiya hadn't had a lot of time with just me—or, maybe I should say, we didn't have enough time with each other. I know that was hard to imagine, considering I would go running to her house early in the morning, but it was true.

Raiya and I were busy, and we liked our own version of busy. She had her GED test prep and work at Rachel's in the morning, while I had work and the SATs and school. It was part of the reason we went well together. But I was determined to make her happy, and to spend as much time with her as I could. (It was limited enough as it was, really.) Especially time when we could be normal teenagers in love. As much as I loved spending time with her, I didn't really want to count trying to save the city as a bonding activity.

As we walked into the shadows of Lakeview Observatory, I pressed the four-point star on my wrist and transformed into my superhero self. Logan was on good terms with "Wingdinger." Or maybe it was Wingdinger that was on better terms with him than Hamilton. Either way, I needed to be able to get information from him, and I didn't think Logan would just up and give it to a mere acquaintance.

"Starry Knight's in the telescope room, talking with Logan," Elysian said. "Or at least she was when I left her."

"Does Logan know her real identity?" I asked. Raiya seemed pretty chummy with Rachel's brother-in-law.

"I don't think so," Elysian said. "Come on, she wouldn't have told you if you weren't going to find out, remember? Do you really think it's likely she would've told Logan?"

"I guess not," I said, as we approached the back door to the observatory. I didn't add that I was just a bit jealous of Logan. He had earned Raiya's respect since the beginning. I'd lost it several times, it seemed, even if I never lost her love.

Before I could ask Elysian what he thought she wanted, a guardsman came out. "You! Stop there," he commanded.

"Excuse me?" I shuffled a few steps back, making sure I was out of his reach. "I'm here on official business."

"You're trespassing," the guard insisted. "This is a restricted entrance." As he seemed to finally register the outfit, he gasped. (Seriously, how did anyone miss the wingdings?) "You're Wingdinger!"

"That's right," I asserted, trying to keep my attention on him, rather than his radio. The last thing I wanted was trouble.

But trouble didn't seem to ever take the hint, especially when it came to this sort of stuff.

The guard frowned and shifted his feet. I knew he was getting ready to charge. "There's a warrant out for your arrest."

He reached for the gun at his belt, and that's when I just reacted instantly, sending a jolt of power straight at him.

Before he could properly cry out, he fell over, unconscious.

I just stared at him. I'd never just attacked someone like that before, let alone a guard. It was too close to the police for comfort.

Elysian let out a guffaw. "You got him! Good aim."

"I hope I didn't hurt him."

"He was going to hurt you, with no qualms."

"Still, he was doing his job."

"Evil 'just does its job,' too, boss. We're allowed to disturb that," Elysian argued.

"Evil has to be intentional," I said, sure I was right. "I'm not sure if it's the same thing as ignorance."

"Willing ignorance is evil."

"Yeah, yeah." I waved him off. "We'll have to discuss it later; I'm not in the mood to discuss the finer points of ethics or philosophy or whatever it is." *At least with Draco's revelation and betrayal, I don't have to worry about Grandpa Odd making me converse with him.*

"Door's open," Elysian said after he used one of his claws to pick the lock.

"Cool."

We headed down the labyrinthine walls, the ones that somehow connected each room and closet. I peeked into the room where the meteorite had been kept prior to its theft; nothing looked any different from the last time I'd seen it.

The fuse box was still melted, and the rest of the display looked untouched.

I stopped for a moment. "Elysian," I said, "the fuse box has been melted. Would Draco be able to breathe fire like you can?"

Elysian snorted. "Of course," he said. "He's always been just as powerful as me. He never explicitly lauded it over me, at least until now. You've already seen how he can transform into people."

"Yeah," I agreed. "But he didn't breathe fire at us while we were fighting him, back when we first found out. Why wouldn't he, if he has such power?"

"Maybe I was right before, and he's not up to full power," Elysian suggested. "That would be my first guess. The second, well, you have to understand, that Draco is a fiercely proud dragon. If he didn't breathe fire when he fought us earlier, it's likely because it wouldn't have been up to his standards."

"But he could still do it?"

"Yes." Elysian nodded, his dragon head bobbing up and down.

"So he must've used the fuse box to disconnect the power," I said. "Just like Logan told me."

"It makes sense, too, because it is older technology," Raiya called out from behind me.

"Starry Knight." I greeted her with a big grin on my face. Quickly glancing over, I saw the lanky shadow next to her. "Logan."

"Nice to see you again, too," Logan said. He had the eager face that came with innocence, and some days I envied him for it. "Starry Knight was just talking about you."

"She was?" I knew the grin on my face turned into a goofy-looking one, and I didn't even care. That much.

"Logan's been able to reconfigure the radiation feed," Raiya told me. "I thought you'd like to see it."

It took me a moment to remember. (There's just so much stuff to recall about this stuff, it was a wonder I could remember any of it at all. Of course, that was where being a genius made a big difference.)

Logan told me before the meteorite had been giving off a strange radiation pattern, one that was a mirror image of the universe's. Almost like an infrablue, he said, instead of infrared. He had every reason to guess that it'd come from outside of our universe. I was more than willing to agree with his conclusion, although I didn't think it was going to help him make his case before the various scientific communities to tell him it had been from a supernova caused by Starry Knight.

In fact, I figured Logan would be laughed at. So I said nothing. It's better to let the facts speak for themselves at times like these.

The meteorite's radiation pattern had also shown up in various parts of town—specifically, in places that seemed to correlate with places where demons of all sorts attacked.

As I glanced over at the map of the city next to the computer reading, I knew all too well which attacks had been at which locations.

"So it's back up and running?" I asked. When the meteorite was stolen, the radiation tracker was disabled.

"Yeah, and it gets better. There's a collection of radiation that's growing just north of the center of the city," Logan said, waxing enthusiasm for his topic, "and the radiation isn't just different, but it's thick. There's a major flux going on, almost like a vortex, collecting the energy and perpetuating itself into … "

I exchanged looks with Raiya as Logan went on with his scientific-sounding spiel. While I liked the guy, and I could appreciate a serious scholar not bent on world domination, this was more or less like one of Mr. Hale's lectures on science stuff I didn't care about, or one of Mr. Elm's chemistry lectures on stuff I only cared about to get me through the SATs.

When I saw what I suspected was a similar expression on Raiya's face, I almost laughed.

"Where is the center of the vortex, Logan?" I asked. "Can you tell me where I could physically see it, maybe?"

"Let me pull up the coordinates on the map," Logan offered.

When a little red blip appeared on the screen, we all focused in on a particular point. A second later, Raiya shook her head. "I should've guessed," she said. "That's where Rosemont Academy was."

"It's being cleared, since Maia more or less managed to bring it crumbling down," I said. "Why would you guess there?"

"Because," Raiya said, "The Skarmastad Foundation was a big donor in making the school as renowned as it was." She shook her head, and after glancing over at Logan, chose the rest of her words carefully. "I got a scholarship. My grandpa said it was a good move, especially since it would let me pursue my interests."

I knew she was thinking of her artwork, and she nodded. It would be a good set up, I thought. Grandpa Odd—Draco— could easily keep tabs on her.

"What happened when the meteorite struck down in front of it?" I asked.

"Grandpa was not happy," Raiya recalled. "I thought at the time it was because he was concerned for me, being upset, but I don't think that anymore."

"Are you guys going to go check it out?" Logan asked. "Do you mind if I come with you? The meteorite might be there, after all," he said. He pushed a stray lock of his black hair out of his eyes, looking at Starry Knight like a hopeful child asking his mother for permission.

"It would be best if you stayed here," I said. I was happy when Raiya nodded. "If there's a lot of radiation, it could mean more of the demons like the one who … hurt you before." I still didn't think "possessed" was the right word. Especially after seeing Elektra and Asteropy hiding out in humans, too. Their minions seemed more like amateur puppeteers playing at power games too advanced for them.

Fortunately, Logan didn't make me explain anything. He just nodded, disappointed but secretly relieved. For a long moment, he almost reminded me of Jason on the night the meteorite crashed into the city.

Raiya patted his arm. "We'll come and check in more frequently," she said, "and we'll bring the meteorite back if we find it."

"Thanks," Logan said, cheering at her message. "The police haven't been terribly helpful, and I at least know that you have an idea of what to look for."

I laughed. "Yeah, the last thing you need is people bringing in fake space rocks for some reward."

Logan grinned. "Exactly."

"What else is going on here?" I asked. I'd failed to mention my attack on the guard to Raiya and Logan, but that didn't mean I'd forgotten it. "How are the Otherworld guards?"

"Tyrannical at times," Logan said with a shrug. "But it's expected, especially since we just got more funding."

"From the Skarmastad Foundation?"

"Yeah. They had insurance on the meteorite, if you can believe it."

"I'm surprised it was covered," Raiya retorted. "Who would cover a piece of rock?"

"It was quite a prize," Logan said, "but it wasn't really enough that the insurance companies would have noticed. The average layman would have no idea it was special."

"What was special about it, besides the radiation?" I asked.

"The metals and substances of it," Logan answered readily, making me suspect he'd thought this over before. "Most meteorites break down because of the heat and pressure from entering the atmosphere. This one did, quite a bit we suspect, but this piece is the core of it. It's awesome, and very strong."

"So basically it's pretty hard to crack?" I asked.

"Yep." Logan laughed. "You'd need some serious heat to melt it down. It's different from any other meteorite or meteor I've ever seen or read about."

"Maybe that's why the Skarmastad Foundation wanted to have it covered," I speculated.

"Maybe."

"And maybe that's why they hired extra people to guard it," I said.

"Most likely," Logan agreed. "But even then, I only found out about the composition a few weeks before it was stolen. They've had extra guards here for nearly a year, or maybe more." He glanced at Raiya. "I was hired here as the main lab coordinator once I entered my second year of graduate school. As long as I can come in and work with no trouble, I usually don't pay attention too much to what happens on a day to day basis."

"Passion has a way of clouding the mundane," Raiya replied.

Logan nodded in agreement, before glancing at his watch. "I'll say. I've got a few grant proposal sheets to fill out. You guys are welcome to stay as long as you can. I wouldn't touch anything, though," he said, looking at Elysian pointedly. "We're pretty conscientious about germs here, sorry."

Elysian grumbled to himself as Logan left. "Spoiled science brat," he muttered.

"Logan's been very helpful," Raiya shot back.

"Hopefully not enough SWORD will notice," I said. "Especially in conjunction with what happened earlier."

"What happened earlier?"

"The kid here was attacked by a guard," Elysian told her.

"He was doing his patrol and he said that there's an arrest warrant out for us," I said. "And so, when he started to look like he was going—"

"You're okay though, right?" Raiya asked.

"Yeah, of course."

"Good." Raiya sighed. "Why would there be an arrest warrant out for us, anyway? Don't you have to be proven guilty?"

"Not if there's suspect," I told her.

"Oh. I guess I should know that."

"I'm here," I reminded her. "I'll take care of the legal side of things." She grinned back at me, giving us a moment of warm comradery.

"What we should know," Elysian cut in, "is what's going on down near your old school, Starry Knight."

"I agree," she said. "But we're going to have be careful about it. Grandpa knows me really well. He'll know what to expect, and he can anticipate it."

"Don't you know him pretty well, too?" I crossed my arms over my chest.

Raiya flushed over red. "I *thought* I knew him," she said. "But we already know the depths of Draco's cunning. I can never be fully sure, when it comes to knowing what he is really like."

I turned to Elysian. "What do you think?"

"I think we should go and check it out before he does something with the meteorite," he said. "He's got his full power, and he in all likeliness has the meteorite, too."

"What can he do with it?" I asked. "I mean, I know he can cause trouble, but I don't have any specific idea."

"Causing trouble is the most specific we can probably get," Raiya said. "We'll need to investigate."

"Speaking of investigating," I said, "I'm trying to find Otherworld. See if we can find its hiring base or something."

"Why?" Raiya frowned. "You know that Dante works for them, but it's just a front for SWORD."

"Draco's been around for a long time," I said. "And he's old enough to have the same weakness as plenty of other older people. He's not as familiar with technology or anything remotely popular."

"What are you talking about?" Raiya asked.

"The Internet," I said. "Otherworld, Inc., as an incorporated business, has to submit documents every year, but I've checked, and there's nothing. No records. I was wondering if they were the connection to the Skarmastad Foundation."

"We already know they are the linked to the Skarmastad Foundation." Elysian huffed indignantly. "They were hired by them."

"But why?" I asked. "SWORD is a global company that's largely a shadow organization. They seek out power to control it. Why would Draco risk his plan—which we can all agree is pretty sadistic—and hire them? Why not just hire a regular bodyguard or a private police force?"

When neither of them could answer me, I said, "There has to be something linking them in more than one way."

"Like the insurance?" Elysian asked. "So he can get more money funneled into his company while still keeping the goods?"

"Exactly." I nodded.

"Maybe Draco's also the head of SWORD," Raiya suggested. "He's the founder of the foundation. Why couldn't he be in charge of SWORD, too?"

"I don't know about that," I said. "I know Dante knows the leader, and he said 'she' when he was talking about her."

"Maybe he hired them to focus on us," Elysian said. "As a distraction."

"That's a good theory," I acknowledged.

"Just be careful," Raiya said. "Grandpa—uh, Draco—told me about SWORD some. He said they were not to be trusted, even if they said they were on our side."

"And yet he hired them?" I asked.

"He's been here a long time," Elysian said. "Maybe he's picked up an additional grudge or two along the way."

I sighed. "This is not getting us anywhere. We need more information."

"Well, that's why you're trying to get it, right?" Raiya said. She nodded toward the door. "Keep us updated. In the meantime, I say we go try and get some information on the vortex Logan found for us."

Elysian frowned. "Let me go," he said. "I'll check it out by myself. Draco wouldn't expect just one of us to show up."

"I'm okay with that," I said. "But you only get to go for reconnaissance. No attacking him."

"Aw, come on," Elysian whined.

"No whining," I added. "We've got to get out of here carefully. We don't need the guards busting in on us because you're being a whiny dragon."

Fortunately, we were able to sneak out without interruption.

As Elysian took off for the Rosemont Academy remnants, Raiya and I stayed behind, watching him take off.

I squeezed her hand. "Hey," I said, glancing over at her.

"Hey, what?" she asked. There was a smile on her face as I reached over and took her hand in mine.

"So, I was talking with Drew today," I said.

"If you're going to ask me about patrolling the city while you have another game night," Raiya warned, "I'm going to tell you no. I don't—"

"It's not that," I assured her. "He was talking about the prom."

Instantly, I could see her body tighten up. "Prom?"

"Yeah," I said. "And I was thinking, it would be kind of fun to go with you. We can finally tell all my friends and the school we're dating, and it'll be the talk of the town for weeks."

"I don't know," she said.

"Come on, it'll be fun."

"Why would you think it'll be fun?" Raiya asked.

"Because you'll be there with me and all my friends and some of yours, and we'll, you know, be normal for a night."

She hesitated. I glanced closer, watching her emotions wisp off her in wavy ripples. Stress, fear, uncertainty …

I stifled a groan. I mean, geez, all that from going to a dance? How did she manage to face down demons and fight off evil with poise and grace, but fall apart at the idea of having fun at prom?

"So are you asking me?"

Her question caught me off guard. "Oh, yes," I said. "I mean, will you go to the prom with me?"

She paused long enough for me to wonder if she would try to wiggle out of it. "Alright." She answered firmly, like she was trying to make up for the lack of enthusiasm.

Luckily, I had enough for the two of us. I took hold of her and twirled her around, before drawing her close to me. "Thank you," I said, before I kissed her soundly. "This means a lot to me. I'll do my best to make sure it's a night you'll always remember."

Raiya laughed, settling into the crook of my collarbone. I could feel how much more content she was as I put my arm around her. I was also more content, as we spent the next few hours walking through Shoreside Park together.

☼4☼
Spawn

As March transitioned into April, while my eighteenth birthday drew closer, and with Cheryl's deadline on death row, Raiya and I regularly met for breakfast after I was done with school. We were even finally able to study together—me for the SATs, Raiya for her GED—something I had been hoping to do for some time. For some strange reason (I hardly ever studied, I hardly ever needed to, and I didn't like to study with other people, so this was new), I was nothing short of sublimely happy.

I should've known it would come to an end.

I should've known it would come to an end.

Maybe I did know, but I was reluctant to admit it.

The first sensation my happy bubble was about to be blown away into pieces of bubble murder—not the exact feeling at the time, but more along the lines of the result—came the first weekend of April.

"What's the formula to figure out compound interest?" Raiya asked as she slumped over her test booklet.

I glanced over. "It's something with a 'p' in it, and a couple of 'n' and 't's,'" I said.

"I know that," Raiya muttered. "I can't remember the order."

"Doesn't your calculator have the automatic function for it?"

"Can't you just tell me the formula?"

"Isn't it on the page of the practice test?"

"No."

"Why do you need it then? Usually those tests give you the formulas."

"I don't see it—"

"Ugh, can't you two just stop talking, period?" Elysian snuggled into the booth we were sharing. He put his claw over his head, dramatically, as if he was going through some kind of fainting spell. "Just look it up and then shut up."

"Are we interrupting your rest, or are you upset I put a cap on your cookie limit?" I asked. "Because you can go back to my house. Or you're free to go on another round of patrols."

"Hey, I've been on enough patrols. You seem to forget who takes care of that sort of thing while you're in school, learning all those facts you'll likely only need if you wind up on a gameshow."

"Considering how you even know about gameshows tells me you've spent way too much time watching television," I said.

"They advertise it in between news reports," Elysian grumbled.

"That doesn't mean anything. You'd actually have to watch them to know what kind of questions—"

Raiya interrupted. "Elysian, stop hijacking my arguments with Humdinger. You know he can't resist arguing with you. Now, he's just going along with it so he doesn't have to admit to me he doesn't know how to find compound interest."

"I cannot believe I ever *wanted* to study with you," I said, half-teasing, half-exasperated. "Here, just give me your paper. I'll write it down."

Several minutes passed as I went through the test question and wrote down the formula for compound interest (which is $P(1+r/n)^{\wedge}(nt)$ for those who don't know).

"There," I said.

"Thank you." Raiya gave me a smile and went to work on the next question. "Maybe one day I'll be able to return the favor."

"I'll keep that in mind." I turned back to my own work, which was less interesting than counting rocks. It was English work. "Actually, what can you tell me about *The Great Gatsby*?"

Raiya put aside her GED math book with a very clear sense of relief. I engaged her services as tutor/entertainer while she told me all about the tragic figure of F. Scott Fitzgerald and his hollow, glamorous life that slipped into sinking madness.

Elysian periodically let out a groan, but he didn't do much more than that.

I didn't mind (much.) Elysian hadn't been lying or even exaggerating—shocker—about going out and checking the town for himself. Ever since Logan had shown us what was happening with the radiation and its swirling signature, we'd been careful to make sure we checked every area close to the old Rosemont Academy building.

So for now, since we didn't see anything, I didn't care. More often than not, I was gratified by my semi-apathy, too, when Elysian or Raiya came back with nothing to report. I never had anything to report either, other than a headache.

True, it was a bit unnerving to worry about Draco. But as the days slipped by, and there was nothing to report, and very little to do, I was growing more sure with each passing day that there was nothing to worry about.

After all, Justice had come to Draco, and she was going to be his undoing, just like the Prince of Stars had said.

Again, I should've known better.

As I was finishing up a sample quiz while sipping the last of my mocha, pain pinched at my wrist.

Immediately, I shook it off. I mean, really, I was better off thinking it was possibly carpel tunnel, since I did type a lot, and working in the silly standardized testing booklet required more writing than I was used to.

Before I could question myself on the matter further, or maybe avoid questioning myself on the matter, Raiya distracted me.

"They're talking about the Flying Angels case on the news," she said, nodding toward the television screen over Rachel's bar.

"Don't pay any attention to it," I said. "Nothing good comes from worrying."

"They're trying to force the police to help capture us," Raiya said.

"Only informally," I said. "I mean, we're fugitives, but you don't see the police careening around the town doing raids."

"Still, it's disconcerting."

"I think it's more than fair to say Cheryl has that effect wherever she goes," I replied drily, not really wanting to worry about my mother.

Raiya's eyes lit up with laughter. "That's true enough."

"Another couple days and we'll be completely in the clear. Cheryl will have to appeal it, and Assistant Mayor Dunbrooke's already told her he has no intention of pursuing it."

"I wonder why."

"Maybe he's talked with Mayor Mills and decided getting too close to it would result in his own hospitalization."

"Or maybe it's just not popular enough of a topic to talk about anymore," Elysian said. "After all, there have been fewer attacks ever since you guys started working together.

They came in random bursts, and now, with the Sinisters defeated, we only have Draco to worry about."

"They know a winning team when they see it," I declared.

Raiya arched her brow and turned her full attention to the screen.

Another burst of pain twisted against my pulse, but I once more pushed it aside. I didn't want to think about it. My SATs were this weekend, and my time to study was limited.

It was growing more limited, too, as I stopped more often than I should have to watch Raiya work.

What is it about really seeing someone? Raiya, as Starry Knight, told me once that I'd seen her, but I wouldn't know her.

Now I did know her, and for some reason it was easier to see her more clearly. As if by loving her, I knew her better, and saw her better, and loved her better because of it.

Some people talk about vicious cycles; I had to wonder what the opposite would be. A virtuous cycle, perhaps?

"What?" Raiya asked, as she glanced over at me.

I put my musings away for the meantime. "Nothing," I assured her. "Just watching you."

"Why?" Raiya glanced over at my practice test materials. "Stuck on the reading section again?"

"No, stuck on you," I told her.

"You know, that might get annoying," she said.

"What?"

"All your attempts at flirting."

"I'm not attempting if I'm succeeding."

"Still, it seems a bit forced."

"Only because I wouldn't naturally do it," I assured her.

"Sure you do," Raiya said. "I remember how you would do this all the time with Gwen."

The nerves around my wrist began to sound off like sirens. I grimaced. "I don't want to talk about Gwen," I said.

"But you flirted with her too," Raiya said. "I'm not bringing it up to make you mad, I'm just pointing out that your time with me is more important to me than your praise."

"I happen to like telling you that you're beautiful," I insisted, still trying to breathe properly while I was in pain. I cleared my throat. "Look, I might've flirted with Gwen while I was dating her, and probably before," I said carefully, realizing that even at my best, this was sounding worse, "but this time I'm with you. It's different because it's you."

She opened her mouth, probably to object, and I shook my head.

"Okay, look, everyone's out there, searching for love, right?" I held out my hands, angry I had to explain myself, but also frustrated I wasn't doing a very good job at it. "Some people try to find it with different people. It's the same with math, you know. You keep trying and adjusting things until you find the right answer."

"Does that make me your right answer then?" Raiya asked.

"Yes." I never hesitated.

She considered it a moment, and then smiled. "I like that better than the cheesy flirting," she said.

"You were the one who taught me that it doesn't count unless I suffer," I reminded her.

"Ugh, you need to write a movie or a sappy love song together." Elysian shifted in his seat. "Or maybe you need to write a book. Though I doubt a lot of people would buy it."

"Even if we included you in it?" I asked.

"Well, maybe," he said. "But you'd have to tone down my awesomeness, or I'd easily overshadow you both, especially if you have too much of that lovey-dovey mushy stuff in it."

I was about to start arguing with him when his nostrils flared. Elysian unfolded himself and slithered around the seat. "Something's wrong," he said.

"What is it?" I asked.

"Can't you tell?" He nodded toward my wrist, where what had begun as a simmer began to boil over.

"Well, um, I just thought maybe since the Sinisters were captured, I was just getting paranoid," I lied.

Raiya narrowed her eyes at me. "You should have said something."

"I didn't want to interrupt our time together," I admitted, somewhat sheepishly.

"Hamilton," she said, "this is too important."

"Can't *you* tell anymore?" I asked.

"Not always," she admitted. "I think it might be because of Grandpa—I mean, Draco. He knew I was sensitive to the monsters and their activity. He would be clever enough to take precautions if he could."

"So, we're both at fault."

She frowned. "Just say something if you feel something next time, alright?"

"Okay, fine," I snapped, tired of trying to impress her and please her. "Next time I'll yell it in the streets for you, too."

"We need to go," Elysian interjected. "So if you're going to fight like an old married couple, let's save it for later, shall we?"

I felt my face turn purple as angry fireballs appeared in my vision.

"We're coming," Raiya said. She shut her books and tucked them into her backpack, and then she reached for mine. "I'll put them upstairs and meet you guys on the roof," she told me.

I said nothing, still sore from her admonishment, only nodding and hurrying off after Elysian.

Elysian was in mid-transformation when I grabbed him by the neck. He choked and gasped. "What?"

"Don't make jokes like that," I scolded. "Raiya and I are *not* an old married couple, and I don't want her thinking that."

"You act like it sometimes," Elysian retorted. "And what's wrong with that?"

I watched as understanding dawned. "Oh," he said, trying to hold back his giggles. "I see! You're worried she won't want to—"

"Shut up," I grumbled, tossing him behind me. We turned down the alley and I pressed into my pounding mark, transforming into my superhero self.

My wings caught me as I jumped up to land on the rooftop. Raiya was already waiting for me, and I was more than pleased to see the feather I'd given her—one of my own burning flame feathers—in its familiar spot, tucked securely in her own bound-back hair.

I landed beside her, already looking around for any sign of an aura.

"There," I exclaimed, pointing off toward the marina. "There's a dull shadow coming up from the docks."

"I see it, too," Raiya said. Worry lined her face. "It's close to Lakeview Observatory."

I glanced over at her, and another aura caught my eye. I frowned and squinted, trying to see if I could discern anything else from it.

It was the vortex, I realized a moment later. It was close to the Rosemont ruin, and it was quietly humming a steady power, while the aura by the marina was erratic and fluctuating.

Before I could say anything, Elysian took off, and Raiya followed. "Hey, wait for me," I called.

"I don't know if it's Draco," Elysian rumbled as I caught up to him. "For all he is evil, he wouldn't leave this much of a demonic trail."

I didn't know what to say to that. While it was true Draco was more dragon than demon, he had captured the Sinisters, and Orpheus, too. They used their powers over their many minions to the point where, when we captured them or subdued them, their shadows still seemed to remain.

"It wouldn't surprise me if Draco *was* causing all the activity," I said. "Especially if he was working his way up to full power, as you surmised months ago, Elysian."

Raiya grimaced as she landed. "I don't think this is his work," she said. "This looks more like the work of a *fenfleal* demon."

A *fenfleal* demon was a rogue demon, one who gained power and worked separately from the Sinisters. I'd worked with a few of them before, so I knew they were tricky to handle. They tended to be more unusual, which, since they weren't following orders, was expected to some degree. But they were just as powerful, if not more so, because of their self-leadership.

As I landed, I tended to agree with Raiya's assessment.

There were three people on the ground, fallen over, their eyes vacant and their bodies still.

I walked over carefully to the nearest one, a man looking close to Mark's age. "Hello?" I shook his shoulder. "Hello? Can you—ugh!"

I'd glanced down to see his wrist was boiling with leaking black bubbles.

"What is it?" Raiya asked, hurrying over. "Oh, my."

"Yeah, it's gross," I said. "I don't know what 'it' is, though."

"It looks like the demon used his mouth to suck out the soul," Raiya said. "He bit the man on the wrist, and he left a mark behind."

I glanced down at my own wrist, to see the Emblem of the Prince. "I guess that's not that uncommon," I said.

"The Prince and the demons don't have the same purpose or motive," Raiya reminded me. "And it's unlikely the Prince would use a pair of fangs to poison you."

"I guess so," I agreed. "I guess they can't help but imitate him in the worst possible ways."

"True enough," Elysian agreed. "You don't need to look far to see that in other areas as well."

"Well, I didn't have to look far to see it here, that's for sure," I pointed out. I dropped the man's arm and shuffled back from the burning black bubbles spitting out of his demon bite.

"Are the others the same?" I asked.

"They should be," a new voice responded.

A creepy feeling shuddered up my spine. Simultaneously, Elysian, Raiya, and I turned around.

And there it was. The demon, the *fenfleal*, was lounging around on the ground. It was long in body, almost like a worm or snake, with no hands and slits for its reddened eyes.

Eyes so similar to Draco's.

"Guys, that can't be … uh, that can't be Draco, right?" I asked.

Elysian snorted as he leered down at our enemy. "No, it's not him," he said. "But he might be a spawn."

Even Raiya looked surprised. "A spawn?" she repeated.

"Yes," Elysian said. "He's been able to take a demon and overtake its sentience."

"I still remain myself," the demon objected. "I am Mahiem; but I will admit Draco's power infusion was a great resource for me."

"Draco's smart enough to figure out how to do it so they don't object, or even think anything's wrong with them," Elysian further intoned.

The worm-snake laughed. "You're not as smart as I figured you would be," he said. "Considering all I know about you from your brother."

Elysian growled impatiently.

"Wait." I pulled out my sword. "Release the Soulfire that you've stolen," I ordered.

"I'll release them," Mahiem said with an evil grin, "if you can defeat me."

"What good is the word of a monster like you?" Raiya asked, stringing an arrow in her bow.

When Mahiem only laughed, I took it as a sign that the fight was on.

"Go!" I called, rushing forward, ready to strike.

Mahiem twisted his long body out of my way, recoiling enough that he managed to strike me in turn.

I bucked against the blow, while Raiya hurried forward. Her bow's sharp edges were out as she swung.

Mahiem ducked and slapped her across the back, her wings catching most of the attack. I felt her pain, but I admired how she shrugged it off, same as she always had.

A whiplash of sparkling energy suddenly hit me hard.

"Ouch!" I grit my teeth together. Elysian wrapped his body around me and sent me a targeted look; I caught the meaning, and tepidly inched forward, out of his protection, but also out of the demon's sight.

"I'll catch you yet!" I heard Raiya cry, glancing over Elysian as she unleashed a slew of arrows at once. The arrows flew up, shining brightly, before winding around and binding him to the ground.

As Mahiem squirmed, I jumped forward from behind him; my sword raised high and then went low, cutting through him with quick integrity.

A whirl of energy whipped around, dissolving the demon's body and sending it into nothingness.

"We did it!" I cheered, watching as the Soulfire he'd consumed trickled back to the people on the deck.

"We're not finished," Raiya said. "Watch it."

"Watch what?" Elysian said. "Is Draco here?"

"No, I mean, watch it, the demon aura." Raiya pointed. "Mahiem's gone, but Draco's power remains."

I saw at once the ghost of a shimmering shadow, as it fluttered past, speeding away toward the vortex. I watched it as it disappeared under the city skyline. And then I blinked, and it was gone.

"This is disturbing," Elysian murmured. "He's using other demons."

"I wonder why," Raiya mused.

"You were the one who said he wasn't up to full power," I said, looking at Elysian. "Is it possible he's gathering more energy to refuel?"

"That's possible," Elysian said. He turned to Raiya. "What do you think?"

When she said nothing, he further pressed her for answers. "Despite all that you might think, you're still the one who knows him best."

"But he lied to me," she shot back, embarrassment flooding her cheeks.

"He didn't lie to you about everything," Elysian argued.

"No, and that makes it worse," she said. Her gaze lowered to the ground. "I can't tell you how often I've replayed it all over in my mind, trying to figure out what was true and what was a lie, and what could've been. It's horrifying."

I stepped up beside her. "Starry Knight's got a point, Elysian," I said.

"Think about what he told you regarding Alküzor," Elysian suggested. "He's unlikely to have lied that much about him, because you would have found out the truth."

"He said that he was trapped inside the fires of the earth," she said. "He said he was always trying to break free, but it would require a lot of power to do it. He also said that Alküzor wanted the power to steal this universe away from Time."

"Thank you," Elysian said. "I know it's hard, but we're going to do much better fighting him if we can anticipate him."

"We could also be playing with fire," Raiya replied. "If we focus so much on anticipating him in one regard, we'll completely miss what he has planned. And Grandpa—I mean, Draco—would jump on that."

"Maybe we can use that to our advantage," I suggested. "If we can make him think we're planning something specific, he'll think he has the advantage."

Raiya hesitated. "He might be able to guess that, too. He knows us well."

"You more than me or Elysian," I clarified.

"I don't know about that," she said. "Elysian's his brother."

"That doesn't mean anything," I assured her. "Adam and I are nothing alike."

"So far as you know," Raiya countered.

"Exactly my point," I told her. "I don't know him well enough to think that he would be like me."

Her mouth dropped open at my admission, and, I would argue, how I scored that point against her. I felt the rush of triumph, and I completely forgot about our earlier argument at Rachel's.

Elysian came to her rescue. "You're not actively trying to destroy your brother." He snorted. "And as annoying as you

67

are, I doubt Adam feels like trying to do away with you, either."

"Fine." I gave up. There's no use trying to reason with people who refuse to see reason. "Let's assume he knows everything, then. Everything, every possibility. What would he be doing, using demons to collect power?"

"Power to set Alküzor free, power to regain his strength, power to separate the realm from Time's power." Raiya counted on her fingers. "Anything else?"

"Wouldn't it be so much easier if you could just ask me?"

At the sound of his voice, we turned. And there he was—his Santa Claus beard, his black robe, and his blood red eyes. I tightened my fingers around my sword. "Draco."

☼<u>5</u>☼
Tests

"Draco!" It wasn't long before Elysian echoed my sentiments on the matter. Elysian hissed and reared back, the horns and spikes down his back shooting up in protest.

Draco only laughed, sounding just like an egomaniac in Grandpa Odd's voice.

I felt rather than saw Raiya stiffen beside me. She straightened a second later, but from Draco's glare, I knew he'd seen her reaction.

"No need to fret," he told Elysian. He raised his hand. Seconds later, lightning flashed from his fist. "Why don't you lie down and relax for a bit?"

"Augh!" Elysian recoiled, unable to dodge the attack; he bore the brunt of it, until it bowled him over.

Raiya leapt into action, her bow out, and I followed her. We'd double-teamed enough demons in past fights, and practiced our striking points. I knew we could take him.

Boom! We met his power in mid-air, the compelling clash of our juxtaposed power hurting my ears as it sang out over the city.

"Augh!" Raiya and I both hollered as throbbing power charged through us, pushing us backward and forward at the same time, suspending us forcibly in our position.

Draco laughed as he poured out more power, keeping us close enough to provoke and far enough away we couldn't attack.

And then, all of a sudden, he thrust us back, and we went flying into Elysian.

"Come on," Elysian grumbled, shaking us off, sending us back up on our feet.

"You foolish children," Draco said, no doubt deliberately mocking me. "You're too far out of your league."

"It won't stop us!" I yelled.

"Too bad." He shuffled back, his cloak billowing. "I'll play the gentleman this time, then."

"You're leaving?" Raiya asked, surprised and appalled.

"Of course." He grinned. "But don't worry. I'll be back."

"Why?" Raiya shouted. "Why keep us in suspense? Why not finish us now?"

"For power, of course." Draco turned to her. "The Prince believes that power is ideally spread out among different people," he said. "And I'll agree with him, especially in a fallen world, for unity is a rare and dangerous thing."

"What does that have to do with you?" Raiya asked.

"The Sinisters, and Orpheus, while I am appropriately grateful for their sacrifices for me to recover my body and my power, their powers were too much for their discipline—or rather their lack of it."

"I'll say," I agreed.

"It didn't help that Time and Memory had managed to place a safeguard on their full power," Draco added.

"That's why you need more power?" Raiya continued, inching forward. I saw her plan at once; no doubt, Draco did as well.

"There's no fun, despite what the movies might say, in telling you what I'm doing," he said, glancing tauntingly at me. "Even though it would be amusing to see you ask. So I'll leave you with this for now: When it comes to collecting power and overshadowing lesser demons, you're completely right about me—and completely wrong."

And with a swish of his cloak, he disappeared into the wind.

Raiya launched out another arrow, but she was a second too late; she caught only the sound on the air as he disappeared.

We stood around where we were, all of us clearly torn between stunning confusion and harrowing indecision.

The sound of clicking cameras and approaching footsteps jolted us out of it a moment later. A few people called out our names and waved to us.

I waved back, awkwardly, my personality still drawn to appeal to the public good, while Elysian turned his back, and Raiya tightened her grip on her bow.

"I miss Aleia," I said. "Stopping time just worked so well for us."

"I wonder what Grandpa meant," Raiya wondered aloud.

"Draco," I corrected her. "And he probably just said that to confuse us."

"He had the upper hand," Elysian said. "He would tell us a half-truth like that to kick us when we're down."

"I don't think he was lying," Raiya said. "He didn't seem like he was lying. And he does enjoy a good riddle."

"What could he mean then?" I asked, beginning to back up as more people began to move over to where we stood.

"I don't know." She grimaced. "That's the inconvenient part."

"How can something be completely right and completely wrong at the same time?" I asked.

"True love can be like that," Raiya murmured softly. I almost didn't catch her words, and I knew why she'd been less than willing to share. She was no doubt thinking of Rachel when she said that, and that thought made me all the more circumspect.

True to my colors, I wrinkled my nose in disgust. "I doubt that has anything to do with that."

Raiya said nothing, only sighing as we took off, barely avoiding close encounters with the pedestrian kind.

Later that night, as I was back in my room "studying" alone, I realized Draco had a way of frustrating us, even if we were getting better at fighting together as a team.

Maybe it was the situation or just how stressful and tiring it seemed, but there were other things that frustrated me, too.

I had the SATs this weekend. I had to get my homework done. I had to go to work. I had to do all this superhero work, and now, with Aleia back with Alora, the media were adding a lot of social pressure against me. I had my brother to worry about, my parents were increasingly distanced from me, and for the first time in my teenage life, that made me worried.

The pressure was mounting, and all I wanted to do was go running.

The door opened behind me. I was relieved when Elysian saw me at work, and then he merely grumbled and left the room.

I turned my attention to the window beside my desk. Night was coming swiftly, coloring the sky with the sharpness of its darkness. There was a violet overcast to the city lights, making the night seem more dangerous.

Of course, it was still a city, I told myself. There were still criminals, and homeless people, and people who needed help, and people who had plenty. There wasn't anything special about it, not really. Every day in town, people fell in love, people broke up, people grew apart. Others would learn, make mistakes, and try again. Some would give up. A few might make it big, while others destroyed things.

I thought about Adonaias, about how he seemed so far away and irrelevant to the ordinary person's suffering, the small voice in my heart asking if that included even my suffering.

I mean, really. How could just "having faith" and "accepting the belief" of who he was really change things?

Life was hard and unfair. That was the way of things. But how could this be the way of things? The angry, cynical part of me said that's how it was, and that was how it would always be.

But even as I turned my lights off and closed my eyes, drifting off to sleep, I knew I was not being fair. There was a lot to consider, much more—maybe too much more—than I wanted to, and I was tired.

I was glad—really, really, really, supremely glad—that in all of Cheryl's crazy diets, she never failed to give up coffee. And there were some insane diets. Since entering high school alone, I'd had to deal with the vegan diet, the meat diet, the sugarless diet, the builder's regime, the kidney flush diet, the root diet, and many, many others. Some of them overlapped.

I was in the kitchen, making my own pot, the first time in what seemed like years, when Cheryl bustled into the room. She wearing her work heels, with her hair pulled back in a flawless knot.

Sometimes my mother was a terrifyingly precise woman. If I didn't know from my own personal experience, I would've thought she was a demon, from how perfect she always seemed to look.

"What are you doing here?" she asked, bewildered.

"I live here," I reminded her bluntly. (Not all of us woke up perfect and perky.)

"I mean, what are you doing here, making coffee?" She tensed, and I could see she was weighing her words carefully. "Don't you usually go out for coffee this early in the morning?"

"Would you prefer if I left?"

"No. I'm just … surprised." She glanced over at the coffee machine. "It'll take less time if you push the start button."

"Oh." I pushed it. "Right."

I leaned back against the counter, while Cheryl stood there, looking at her phone and her watch.

THE STARLIGHT CHRONICLES

"It's almost the last day," she muttered unhappily.

"The last day? Of what?"

"The Flying Angels case." She frowned, the lines in her face crinkling disapprovingly. "I miss Stefano," she admitted. "He would have given me more time to get those superheroes in custody."

"I'm sure," I agreed, thinking of Stefano's Sinister-influenced bloodlust. "I suppose Dunbrooke is less lenient?"

"Lenient?" Cheryl scoffed. "Ha! That's a poor choice of words, even for you, Hamilton."

"Sorry … ?" I shrugged. "Martha told me that it wasn't likely that the city would indict them, anyway."

"It could have made my career," Cheryl snapped.

"Really?" I felt a rush of anger hit me as the coffee brewed and my mother stewed. "You would've wanted to be known as the legal form of a political tool who tried to bring people who were helping the city to so-called justice?"

Cheryl blinked, shocked and angry, blindsided by my words. "What are you saying? You wanted to help with the case."

"I did," I agreed, "and having seen it, and its near end, I can say I think it's terrible. That Dante person is terrible, and Stefano was obsessed about the whole thing. It didn't help him any, unless it made him look good to voters and his reelection campaign managers."

"Of course!" Cheryl fumed. "But it opened doors for us. For you, and for me."

"For what?" I shouted back. "So we could hold our heads up and look down on the crumbling ruins of the city?"

"We could've made a name for ourselves."

"You've already made one," I assured her. "My friends all know you. This city already knows you. You have a solid reputation."

"Don't you want one?"

"Not like this, and not like that," I said.

She calmed down, straightening her shirt. "I don't suppose this is because I didn't stay home with you as you grew up?" she asked. "Because I didn't mother you as much as you would've liked?"

"What? What are you talking about?" I cringed. "No. That has nothing to do with this—and that has nothing to do with anything. *This* is about right and wrong. The case was wrong from the start. It wasn't bad just because people don't want to consider the supernatural."

"It was bad because it caused a lot of damage to the city. There are still people who are affected by it. Your own friends are in the hospital because of those so-called superheroes."

"Those so-called superheroes are the only ones who were able to stop the demons from sucking out more souls," I insisted. "It's not my fault, or their fault, that any of those people are still in the hospital."

Cheryl narrowed her gaze. "You didn't think this before," she said. "Has it been that girlfriend of yours who's poisoned your mind against me?"

I didn't bother to tell her that I had thought it before, I just didn't tell her. "I'm not arguing against *you*," I said, throwing my hands up in exasperation. "I'm arguing against your stance and your underlying perspective." I almost roared at her, hoping to leave Raiya out of this, that she had nothing to do with this, but I knew that wasn't entirely true.

"Do you even want to be a lawyer anymore, Hamilton?" Cheryl asked me. "You're living in a fool's world. We don't live in a black and white world, where there's such thing as 'right' and 'wrong.'"

"Just because a lot of people say there is no 'right' answer and no 'wrong' answer doesn't mean that they're right," I said. "That's the majority fallacy. And anyway, as lawyers, we're only concerned with the law, and the ambiguity between theory and practice."

She stared at me for a long moment. "If you really believe that," she said, "you're going to have a hard time being a lawyer."

"Why?" I asked. "Are ethics and morality dead?"

"It's easier to do the work if you believe they are at least on life support," she said. "Idealism is never a good path, Hamilton. Disappointment can be harsh."

"Life is harsh," I said. "But there are still things worth living for."

"You're too young to know that."

"No, I'm not!"

"Yes, you are." She shook her head. "You only know what's worth living for when you've found something worth dying for."

"Dying for something is easy!" I yelled back. "It's *too* easy! Living for something is harder."

"You've changed, Hamilton." She sighed. "This is because of your girlfriend, isn't it?"

"You leave her out of this," I snapped. There was no way I was going to admit she was right—well, partially right, anyway. There were other reasons I'd changed, too; Raiya just happened to be one of the bigger reasons why.

"I'm only asking because I'm concerned for you," Cheryl insisted.

It always amazes me in life how the people who say they are "trying to help" are usually the ones who are doing the most damage. It is almost like a red-flag phrase.

"I'm not worried," I lied.

"What are you going to do?" Cheryl shook her head. "You want to be a lawyer at Pitt still, right?"

"Of course."

"Is she going to just move with you to college? You don't know what she wants to do, do you?"

I said nothing.

That was a mistake; I should've lied, fast and immediately. Cheryl knew the real answer at once, and she began to milk it for all it was worth.

"What about her family? Is she going to leave them to go with you? How are you going to provide for her? I know from paying all your bills, you couldn't afford standard rent *and* your coffee habit. And if she stays here while you go off to school, how do you know she won't find someone else? That she won't find a job here or far away from here that she'll want?"

"That's none of your business."

"I'm just trying to make sure you know what *you're* doing. You need good grades and high scores on your tests to get scholarships and awards and prizes, Hamilton."

"Have I *not* been doing that?" I asked.

"Technically, you have done that. But lately, I see you're distracted." She shrugged delicately. "You're going to need to change that if you're still working toward dual enrollment next year."

The coffee machine beeped, probably saving me from screaming at Cheryl until the rest of the neighborhood woke up.

I swore I could almost hear Elysian chuckling at the picture I made.

I poured a cup into one of the many hundreds of coffee thermoses we had around the house. "Well, I have my SATs today," I said, abruptly changing the subject. "Let me go ahead and show you how *not* distracted I am."

I shoved the coffee pot at her and turned away, secretly hoping I'd managed to spill some drops on the counter just to tick her off.

Getting outside the door was walking into the very essence of sweet relief, even if I was headed out to take a test on a Saturday.

The chilly morning air reminded me that there was still some talk of snow coming, even in April, but the steaming cup in my hand shut that possibility up.

At the bitter taste, I suddenly wondered why I hadn't gone to Rachel's. It was true that since it was Saturday, she wouldn't have been open until seven, the same time as my test, but I could've managed to get a cup out of Raiya.

I looked down at my cup, seeing past the coffee-colored liquid joy to see my own reflection, and I knew.

I was still feeling unsettled about yesterday.

I didn't want to fight with Raiya. At least, not to the point where I hated her for her remarks.

I didn't even know *why* I was bothered by our argument. Sure, maybe I should've said that I was sensing a demon attack. But my reluctance to ruin our time together should've redeemed my poor judgment in the matter.

Well, I decided silently to myself, *poor judgment yesterday doesn't qualify for a follow-up today.*

I decided I would go and see her immediately after my SATs were over. I had four hours to take the test, and then I would be done. Maybe I would even feel better to the point where I would welcome some demon-fighting action.

I can't imagine sitting in a desk chair on a Saturday for a good half of a school day is something a lot of students gleefully anticipate.

SATs, the standardized college tests, were a legacy of the twentieth and twenty-first centuries. Even as I sat down for mine, I had a feeling they would either go away or they just get more complicated in time. I thought it was hard to argue for them, generally speaking, but it was harder for schools to look for another way to get a kid's parents to shell out a considerable sum in order to look good on a college admission packet.

Cheryl was right, for once, about college and dual enrollment. I needed that in order to skip through the first year of college, which I knew from my own investigations was similar to my high school classes. It was possible if I did well enough, I could graduate from law school by the time I was twenty-one.

Raiya had joked, when I told her, that it was perfect, since I could start my career the same time it was legal for me to become an alcoholic. I smiled at the memory. I wasn't worried about law school. I'd succeeded in school stuff all my life. It wasn't hard for me to learn.

It was the physical toll on me that I was less enthusiastic about, and the SATs were goading me more there than anything else. Actually succeeding into college clearly required the ability to sit and wait for an hour, and then sit, answer questions, and then wait for another hour or two, all while having no access to the internet; I'm sure making the money from the testing fees was just a perk for colleges.

Other than that, the test wasn't hard for me. I was done with each section with tons of time to spare, and no Game Pac or phone or anything to play with. I had to fight off the temptation to bother Jason, who was just a row over from me; though, in all fairness, it would've been a short-lived endeavor, since he was taking his precious time.

Poncey was a couple rows over from Jason, but he couldn't see me very well. It wasn't like he could turn around without one of the testing proctors getting angry, anyway.

My desk was next to the window, and that was seriously the only entertainment I could enjoy. And the horizontal blinds were halfway shut, making it all the more enjoyable.

[Insert sarcastic eye roll.]

It was boring and I don't remember much, only staring into space for hours, and then looking up at the clock to see approximately two minutes had passed, and then repeating this a bunch of times. I also remember glaring at the clock, and mentally yelling at Aleia to speed things up for me.

Surely she wouldn't deny me that request? She was a friend, after all.

Adonaias probably wouldn't let her, I thought an hour-long moment later.

There is absolutely nothing *worse that this—*

My train of thought was derailed and ran into a barn silo as searing soreness clasped around my wrist.

Again?!

I almost cried out an overly-clichéd long, drawn-out "No!" If there was any appropriate time to do just that, it was at that moment, while I was sitting with an hour to go on my SAT writing test, and demons were working in all their terrible ways.

Glancing out the windows, I could see next to nothing, other than the other wing of the school building. I was in a different classroom than my normal routine, so even Elysian would have a harder time finding me.

Raiya, I knew, had opted not to take the SATs. She decided to worry about her GED test first, and then she said, she would "worry about college when and if the time came." I

THE STARLIGHT CHRONICLES

assured her, in my typical, unfeeling fashion, that it was a matter of "when."

College had been a mandate on my life for forever. Now that she was a part of my life, it was one on hers, too.

There was a loud *crash!* that sounded from out the window.

But fighting off the demons, and all of their leaders and masters, was also a calling on my life.

Instant frustration ran through me. I felt like Draco did this on purpose, like he had been working in secret conjunction with Cheryl. Her challenge to me this morning burned into my mind, making me hate my mother and life and everything else all the more as I faced brutal reality. I could taste blood as I contemplated revenge.

I did this while I remained in my seat.

I let the pulsations of pain and suffering slither through me like a poison, seeping from my wrist down to my heart and infiltrating my mind.

Never did I feel the demand on myself so much as when I sat there, writing my essay, reading through questions, figuring out math problems—all while my friends were called to the battlefield.

I glanced at the clock.

Come on, Alora, stop time for me so I can help … Aleia, tell Alora to help me!

When I got no response, I turned to a higher power. *Adonaias, where are you? Answer me! Go help Raiya and Elysian! What could you possibly be doing that matters as much as this does right now? Why aren't you helping them?! Why are you keeping me here?!*

Nothing.

I got nothing.

Minutes passed. I could hear sirens and screaming. I could hear buildings buckle. At one point, I felt the shockwave of an attack. My heart twisted in agony, and I wondered if Raiya was doing okay.

But I did nothing.

I couldn't leave. I mean, I *really* couldn't. Not without cancelling my scores, forfeiting my testing fees, and losing my chance for dual enrollment at Apollo City College next year! This was the last testing session they had before my application had to be in. Even if I took the test again, it would be too late to apply for the program.

There was also the matter of my mother. If I left, I would be proving her point—that I was focused on other things besides my long-term success.

Not to mention, I rationalized, I could easily draw suspicion to myself and Wingdinger, if someone were to realize the connection between my disappearances and Wingdinger's appearances. Gwen had been quick enough to pick up on it, hadn't she, months ago? And she was quick enough to use it against me, too.

So I did nothing.

All my conflicting panic stymied me, stilling me, trapping me in my chair.

I was only slightly comforted by the fact no one else who was around did anything. I could see the confusion on the faces of the testing coordinators. Some of them asked questions over their radios, but there was no change.

All of us in the room were told nothing—nothing other than what to do, how to answer questions, how to pack up our materials, and when to expect our scores.

The dam of confusion and anger broke the instant we were allowed to pack up and leave.

A hand clasped me on the shoulder. "Dinger!" Poncey called. "What do you say?"

"To what?" I snapped.

"To going to my house, kicking back, and playing some video games? I got Drew and Simon coming," he said, clearly unaware of my inner turmoil. "They're going to bring over some—"

I shook my head quickly, interrupting him. "No." I pushed him away. "I gotta go."

"But—"

"*I gotta go*," I repeated brusquely, emphasizing each word, like he was unable to understand me.

He had a hurt expression on his face, and I felt my frustration compound itself further inside of me.

But I brushed it off. I had to. I had to go.

"Augh!"

I winced at the sound of Elysian's cry; I was flying over the old Rosemont Academy grounds as I saw him slump down against the ground, defeated not entirely in his body, but somewhat in his spirit.

I shook my head, which is a bad idea to do mid-flight, and tried to reassure myself it was not too late to make a difference. There was a price to be paid when it came to making difficult choices.

Raiya, transformed into Starry Knight, was fighting with Draco in his human form. His energy crashed against hers as they edged closer to the vortex.

"Hold on," I yelled, probably more to myself than to either Starry Knight or Elysian. "I'm coming!"

The aura around the battlefield was deadly dark; I could see the demonic spirits swirling around inside the core of the vortex.

I landed beside Elysian and put my hand up to his scaly cheek. "Are you okay?" I asked.

His jaw snipped at me, as angry smoke came rushing out. "What took you so long?!" he yelled.

"I had my test today. I couldn't leave."

Elysian roared at my words. He blew a string of fire out of his mouth as his body snapped back into action, his will sharpened by his anger.

Even if it was because he was angry with me, it was good to see him moving.

But it was not good to see the fire stirring. The vortex grabbed up the celestial fire he unleashed, spinning in faster circles with flames leaping up out of the mix.

"What's happening?" I called, keeping up beside Elysian as he hurried over to dodge a spurt of his own power.

"My power is mixing with the demon remains," he explained. "We need to make sure it doesn't spread!"

I glanced at the fire. How was I going to stop that? My power would likely cause more trouble for us. *Would my sword work?*

Doubt burned into me, as the flames grew hotter.

"It's nice of you to finally join us," Draco said to me. "You're just in time for the big finale." Calling forth his power, Draco squeezed it into his palms, gathering it up together in one big energy ball.

I stepped forward, my sword out and ready. "I'm the one who just got here, and I'll decide when the show's over—"

Draco didn't wait. He unleashed his power; it circled around me, before trapping me in a deadly spiral.

"You … won't … win," I said, gasping as his power met mine. The sword in my hands shook from the pressure. I could feel my power bend around me, protecting me, but I was unable to move forward against the surging tide.

I caught sight of Raiya and Elysian; both were struggling in the power fields, the same as me.

Draco's cold laughter forced my attention back to him. His power continued to grow as the vortex opened up to reveal its heart—or rather, what was lying at its heart.

A strange but familiar rock was there, glowing with a blueish shimmer.

It was the meteorite!

The same one that had smashed through the Rosemont Academy streets, the same one that had blown up as it was being moved to a lab, and the same one Logan had kept watch over for all those months at Lakeview Observatory.

I watched as the meteorite burned away, the shadow of Elysian's flames and the darkness of the demonic aura reforming its shape.

The power binding me slowed, and I was able to wriggle into a weak spot. Seconds later, I felt a rush of jubilee. "I'm out!"

THE STARLIGHT CHRONICLES

"Watch out!" Raiya called to me as she was pushing through her own bonds.

I jerked my sword up just in time to stop another round of Draco's energy. "I can't hold out forever!"

Draco's red eyes pierced me through the wall of flames between us. He opened his mouth, and for a moment I thought he was going to laugh or gloat again.

I was wrong.

A burst of fiery lightning erupted out of Draco's mouth, scorching the skies and mixing with Elysian's fire in the demonic pit. Power unleashed upward, cutting its way through clouds.

It was loud and terrifying and I wished I'd had earplugs. A foreboding hum electrified through me. My skin crawled with light and chaos, as my ears closed up at the frightening force.

"No!" I saw, rather than heard, as Elysian cried.

When I could see again, the only things I could make out clearly were Draco's smile, and the newly-transformed meteorite.

It was no longer a rock, but a weapon of power and shadow; the dragon fire combined with the pressure of the vortex had forged a sword.

As the vortex disappeared, Draco reached out for his prize. He grabbed it by the hilt, and it was at once remade, colored with the emptiness of his soul. The power holding me back, the power holding Elysian and Raiya back, disappeared.

"Excellent," he hissed.

The vortex was suddenly gone; even the road seemed to fix itself, emptied of the demonic power it once held.

Fully released from Draco's power, Raiya fell forward onto her knees, clearly spent.

"Stop him before he gets away!" Raiya called to me.

I didn't even stop to think; I knew she was right. Elysian and Aleia had warned me before that objects such as the meteorite could be used to cause further damage, and its power would magnify when used to further evil's cause.

That had to be it!

He'd used the vortex as a dumping ground for calamity, and used the fire and power provided to meld the meteorite into an even deadlier weapon of choice—one that could counter our attacks and serve an even darker purpose.

Our swords met and clanged, sending a tremor through my body. Lightning flared out from our swords, as mine attempted to seal away a sword of nothingness.

"Ouch!" He managed to score a lucky swing, and I tumbled to the ground, cursing my delayed defense.

His eyes narrowed in grim pleasure as he lifted his sword over me, preparing to deal me another blow.

I braced for it, calling my power up to shield me. My eyes squeezed shut, bracing for the impact.

Nothing came; I heard nothing other than a quick intake of breath.

Glancing up, I saw him glaring at the arrow of light sticking through his shoulder.

Behind him, I saw Raiya shaking. She'd broken free, and her bow was out; she had a despondent look on her face.

Draco surprised us both by grinning. "*Tsk, tsk,*" he told her as he jerked the arrow right out from his body. The purity of Starry Knight's power had decimated a hole right through him, but a second later he healed himself. "I thought I taught you better than that, Raiya."

Raiya looked as shocked as I felt. I knew intimately what kind of power she was capable of wielding. What happened? And why wasn't she shooting another arrow?

"But it's an improvement from the last time we met," Draco drawled on. "I'll have to work around that."

I shot out my own power at him, hoping with his attention diverted that he would be vulnerable.

No such luck, of course.

After dodging my attack, Draco laughed and faded away. His voice whispered past my ear as he left.

"Parting is such sweet sorrow, is it not, young Hamilton?"

His words echoed inside of me, taunting me, making me flustered and frustrated.

What did he mean by that? I wondered.

Of course, I had to wonder if it meant anything at all. Clearly, it was an insult of some kind, I get it, but insults don't usually have hidden meanings in them. They were just insults.

The scene of the fight cleared, and I was left, still hunched forward, my sword limply held up in my wrist, standing alone, unable to get over the meaning or the final message.

"Well," I said as I allowed myself to regroup, "that was weird."

Raiya and Elysian stepped forward. I turned to face them, knowing they would be disappointed.

"Good job, kid." Elysian snorted. "Now he's got a sword, and one that has a considerable amount of power, too."

I frowned. "It's not like I could've stopped him from leaving," I argued. "He just disappeared into nothing."

"We might have been able to stop him if you'd gotten here earlier," Raiya said.

It took me less than a second to wheel around. "Excuse me? You were the one who clearly hesitated here!"

"What do you mean? I managed to get him!"

"You told me once your power allows you to hit any target you want. Why didn't you get his heart?"

"You know why!" she shouted.

"Well then, it's both our faults at best that he got away!"

"We still might have a better chance if you'd gotten here earlier," she repeated, this time with more anger than I'd been expecting.

"I couldn't get here any sooner," I declared. "And at least I got here after the SATs finished up."

"Is that why you were late? Seriously?!" Raiya stepped forward. "I can't believe you! We just talked about this yesterday."

"Hey, it's one thing for me to keep quiet because I wanted to spend my time with you," I replied, "and it's another thing for me to ruin my chances at dual enrollment next year. I have to consider the future. Once Draco's defeated, our mission will be complete, and we'll be able to return to our regular lives."

"You know how important it is that we protect this city," Raiya argued. "There won't be a future if you don't work for it!"

"Exactly my point," I shot back. "I won't get into college if I don't take these tests seriously."

"These tests are secondary to survival," Raiya shot back. "You're risking that on the chance we actually succeed! Why are you so eager for your time as Wingdinger to be over?"

"Because I actually have a life separate from him, unlike you!"

She looked stricken, as though I'd struck her, and I knew instantly I'd made an unfair argument.

But ...

I also had a point, as painful as it was for her to admit.

"Come on, Raiya. I have a life separate from this," I said again, "and frankly, I like it."

Her eyes lowered, and I cringed.

"I don't consider you separate from my normal life," I quickly explained. "You're the best thing in my life. But don't you like just hanging out, you know, talking about school and college and the future, or even talking about stupid things, like the terrible shows on TV and how ugly someone's new haircut is it just how awful it is waiting to grow up?"

"If you have to ask me that," Raiya said, "it's clear that you haven't grown up."

"I'm not even an adult yet," I said. "It's easy for you to say, because you're eighteen."

"I'm not talking about age!" Raiya folded her arms across her chest. "I'm talking about maturity. You have seen things, things not just anyone has seen. You know better. And you still choose the temporary things over the eternal."

"That's because the temporary has an effect on the eternal!" It was my turn to glare at her. "If you can't see how this matters to me, you have some nerve saying you love me."

"Real mature," Raiya muttered. "I suppose you're going to stomp your foot and march out of here with your nose up in the air?"

"Maybe I will!" I huffed indignantly and then decided she was right.

I left.

☼6☼
"Discussions"

I left, but it didn't take long for the guilt to settle in. Our fight had rocked me, shaken me up to the core, and I felt the emptiness inside quickly being replaced by shame.

Ignoring things that bothered me had become a problem in the time I'd been roped into working the superhero gig. I mean, it wasn't like I could talk to just anyone about it. After all, who would allow you to complain about your duties and *not* report you? I doubted even the most legally conscious therapists would find a way to spill the beans if they wanted.

There is a downside to ignoring things, though, and most of it has to do with sleep.

It's much harder to ignore things when even sleep won't let you forget them.

That night, I felt terrible. I woke up from dreams too unreal, and too real to be unreal. All I could think about was Draco pulling the sword out of the space rock, like some kind of demonic King Arthur on a mission to destroy the world.

As morning came and attempts to sleep slowed, I could hear the soft drizzling of April showers as raindrops flowed down my bedroom window.

It wasn't long before all I wanted to do was go see Raiya, sit in the café, and listen to her talk while I drank coffee. But I wasn't sure she would let me in, and that doubt was enough to keep me tucked underneath my bed covers.

After all, I'd managed to insult her quite a bit, adding injury to more injury from our previous argument on the matter.

And I had let Draco get away with his new weapon, which was going to make defeating him much harder, no doubt.

But most of all, I'd shown my hand; I had allowed my normal life to take precedence over our supernatural calling.

Can you still love someone, even if they make bad choices? Break promises? Take selfish risks?

Of course you can. It's just probably not the wisest thing in the world to remain associated with them.

I was so sure Raiya would agree with that. So I avoided her.

I continued to avoid her through the rest of the weekend. She called and texted me, but I ignored her. I didn't even go to Rachel's. I went to Poncey's instead, and played video games longer and louder than the rest of my friends.

Monday came. School was less than exciting, but it kept me busy and safe from Raiya and her eventual rejection.

I was only able to wake up from my self-pity stupor when Martha caught my attention as class finished up. I turned in my reading questions on the chapter in the Supreme Court, and she whispered to me, "I found them."

A long moment passed before I remembered I'd asked her to help me find Otherworld. We had unfinished business to attend to, and I was not going to give up on it just because I didn't feel like taking care of it. "Really?"

"I wouldn't lie to you, Dinger." Mrs. Smithe scowled.

"Sorry." I shrugged. "Not used to asking for help. What can you tell me?"

"I found Otherworld," she said. "I got in touch with an old contact. Most of them are contracted workers staying around the city in hotels."

"What does that mean?" I asked. "It sounds like a lot of work, if we have to search out all the different hotels."

I thought of the time Aleia, Elysian, and I managed to find one of SWORD's black sites. It was in a hotel, too; I guess since that particular incident, they'd spread their forces out among the city.

"It's not like that," Mrs. Smithe insisted. "Otherworld, Inc. is a new company."

"That would explain why I couldn't find any tax documents online," I said.

"It's a common enough name," Mrs. Smithe told me. "It's the name of several businesses and organizations that have worked in different parts of the world. Many, if not all, have closed or have been bought, sold, and rebranded."

I recalled some of the conspiracy theories I'd seen about the company. I paused for a moment before I asked my question. (Does anyone *really* want to learn a truth that's world-shattering?)

"What does this mean?"

I was a bit disappointed when she didn't confirm any conspiracy theories.

"It's a front," she explained. "Its current address is a P. O. box, located in the Time Tower downtown."

"That's the headquarters of the Skarmastad Foundation," I said, as I suddenly remembered.

"The leader of this current taskforce is staying in Lake County Heights."

I groaned to myself. She had to be talking about Dante. (He was their lead guy? *Really?*) "I know. He's staying at the house down the street from me."

"If you knew, why did you need my help?"

Good question. "I thought it would help," I admitted. "I didn't think of trying to ambush him."

"It's better if you take him out." Martha's eyes were uncharacteristically dark as I looked at her. "Before they take you out."

"Well," I said, suddenly feeling like I had made a big, huge mistake, "I don't want to get SWORD on my *complete* bad side."

I decided not to mention how Dante was determined to protect me, as he saw me as the key to defeating the bad guys.

"There is no such thing as their good side, Hamilton," Mrs. Smithe said. "Morally ambiguous people have already compromised themselves. They'll ditch you once they have what they want."

"What could they possibly want from me, other than to stop the demons running around the city?" I asked, keeping my voice as soft as I could.

"There's no way to know all the time," she said. "But you can assume it's something bad."

"I'll try to keep an open mind about it."

"I'm serious." Mrs. Smithe admonished me, her lips tightening even more than usual. "They've been around for decades now. They're good at their business."

"What did you do for them?" I asked.

"I don't want to talk about it." She shook her head. "You wouldn't believe me if I told you, and I don't want you to know. They're good at keeping their secrets."

"I guess that's true." I thought of Dante's face, when I first told him I knew about Mikey. He was shocked, or so I thought. Now that I knew him a bit better, I realized he was more than shocked; he was terrified.

"You'd better keep your word."

I glanced back at Martha, uncertain for a moment of what she meant.

She looked over her glasses frames, eyeing me intently. "You can't talk to me about this again. It'll be trouble for us both."

I nodded. "Thank you for your help. I'll see what I can do to use it well."

"I'm glad to hear it." She gave me a half-smile. "Be careful out there, Dinger. I have faith in you, but you're up against a formidable enemy."

Having Martha's approval stunned me, awed me, even humbled me. As I watched her take another swig of her coffee, I felt a rush of gratitude for the small lady who suffered so much to teach me what she knew; I had a feeling she taught me more about honor and courage than history and government.

"I will do my best," I promised, and maybe for the first time, I actually meant it.

"Good. Now, skedaddle. You're going to be late for your next class."

Despite all the warm feelings, I was unsettled by the conversation I had with Martha. So far, SWORD had seemed more like an ally than an enemy. True, Dante had a large role in Taygetay taking Gwen's Soulfire. And they had tried to capture us before ... and Dante was on Cheryl's side when it came to our legal disputes.

There was also the fact that Raiya believed them to be against us.

But wasn't that how things often worked? Two sides would come together to defeat the greater evil?

Surely even Martha would know that, considering she taught history for a living.

I respected these women in my life, and I knew they had a good record of being right. Of course, that didn't mean that they were automatically right, but their conclusions were discomforting.

On the bright side, Martha's information did force me to go and see Raiya once school was out. I'd thought about trying to avoid her for a couple more days, giving my self-righteousness some time to both calm down and strengthen itself for her fury. But Martha's insight, coupled with her pragmatic relentlessness, seemed to warrant discussion.

And I knew that, even if Raiya wanted to step back from me, she was stuck with Wingdinger as her co-defender and Starlight Warrior companion.

After the bell rang, I hurried down the hallway and headed out to Rachel's. I coasted through, my mind and mouth coordination in a dance I seemed to be born knowing; I skimmed through my friends' catcalls, parried their jabs, and echoed back their whoops. (I didn't even know what they were saying, but they were always relatively low-maintenance followers.)

By the time I got to the street, seeing Raiya again remained my only focus; she was the Ritalin to my life's ongoing ADD.

As I stepped inside the café, I suddenly had to wonder if Elysian wasn't there as well; I knew he'd spent a lot of time with Aleia while she was with us, and he seemed to like our other teammates more than me (the feeling was mutual, I assure you.) I certainly hoped he'd stayed at my house, avoiding the maids as they cleaned and Ayako while she cut up her dead fish.

Of course, that was probably a good reason why he *wouldn't* want to be there.

"Hamilton," Rachel called out from behind the bar. "Nice to see you again."

"Always nice to see you, too, Rachel," I said. The pretty barista's greeting calmed me as much as the coffee she gave me re-energized me.

She handed me one of her newer concoctions—a cupcake filled with a fruit and yogurt parfait mix—before nodding toward the back stairs. "Raiya's upstairs, if you're looking for her," she said. "She said she wanted to go out today, so she'll be down soon."

"Thanks. This looks great," I said. I held up the crumbly cupcake.

"How was your test?" Rachel asked. "Raiya told me that you slept all weekend after taking it."

"Uh, yeah, totally," I said. "It was exhausting."

"I guess so, if you weren't even here this morning."

I frowned. "How did you know I wasn't?" I asked.

"I've been coming in some mornings," Rachel said, "ever since Grandpa disappeared."

"Oh."

"Raiya's been distressed about it." Rachel sighed. "Of course, I can't believe he's gone, either."

I thought about Draco and his long-term undercover act; he'd been settling here for decades, waiting for her to show, and setting up a web of interests and businesses long before his grandfather persona took the stage. Before that, he played Ogden Skarmastad, the city founder and the founder of the Skarmastad Foundation, and turned out to be a sadistic form of evil incarnate, who transformed himself several times throughout his long, immortal life. Who knew how many other lives he had before that?

"Maybe he'll come back," I said, trying to be kind to Rachel, even if the inauthenticity of my tone nullified most of my efforts.

"I hope so," Rachel said. "But in the meantime, I'm trying to step up and help around here more. Jason's been here a lot more, too."

I hadn't noticed that, either.

"I know Raiya has her GED to pass, and Mom is not the most willing worker, even if it is our family income," Rachel continued.

"I could tell," I assured her, recalling Letty's perpetual pouting. I dreaded the days I would come in and she would be working. Grandpa Odd had weirded me out, but Letty's displeasure made it seem like I was an inconvenience. I felt bad she was also watching Adam for me a couple of times a week, although I didn't know if I should feel worse for Adam or her.

"That's an understatement. But I appreciate your restraint."

"Are you doing okay?" I asked. "I mean, I know you're concerned for Raiya, but you have to keep track of yourself and the others in your family now."

"Lee's been fine. He and Grandpa weren't really close," she said. "Logan's been more morose, but that's because he's still sad that the meteorite of his has gone missing and he won't be able to continue his research."

I laughed. "That sounds like Logan, from what Raiya's told me."

"She likes going there to see him," Rachel said. "I'm wondering if she won't go into astronomy, too. A lot of her paintings have a cosmic theme behind them."

I glanced at the door, where the painting Raiya had given Rachel for her wedding still hung. It depicted the scene from the legend of the Weaving Girl and the Herder Boy, who married and loved each other so much they neglected their duties. They were separated, only allowed to visit each other once a year, and they became stars in the sky, positioned across the Milky Way.

"Maybe." I turned back to Rachel. "I'm sure whatever she decides to do, she'll surprise me."

"I think it's easier when you've known what you wanted to do for a long time," Rachel replied. She gestured around the café. "I graduated college, took out a business loan, and set up shop here. And while we're still making payments, this is my home."

"Yes, it is." I nodded. "I also agree with you, about wanting to know what you want to do. I was practically born wanting to be a lawyer."

"You've been looking for justice all your life, huh?" Rachel asked. There was a smile on her face as she said it, and I knew she was teasing me.

She was right, of course. I had literally been looking for justice all my life, to the point where I'd fallen in love with its living incarnate.

"I guess so," I finally replied. I tightened my grip on my cup as I finished the cupcake. "This was great, as usual, Rachel."

"Thanks!" She glowed contentedly.

"I'm going to go check in on Raiya," I said, "but I might want seconds before I leave."

"Don't you always?" Rachel laughed and waved as she picked up my dishes and carried them into the kitchen.

I hurried up the stairs and knocked on Raiya's door. After a moment of silence, I twisted the knob, surprised to see it was unlocked, and peeked in.

"Raiya?"

THE STARLIGHT CHRONICLES

It took me less than a moment to realize why she hadn't answered. She was painting as she listened to music.

I was surprised to hear her sing. Her voice was soft and deep, a comforting alto rather than a smooth soprano. Observing her even further, watching her frown and examine each stroke of her brush, and smile when she was satisfied, I couldn't help but think she would make a good mother.

I came up beside her, standing beside a familiar case, the one I recognized from the school play last year; it was, as usual, stuffed with different paints and supplies.

Leaning over, I placed a quiet kiss on her cheek. I felt a rush of guilt when she pulled back, stirring her out of her song.

"You can keep going," I said. "I'll wait for you."

"I need to stop, don't worry," she said. Raiya pushed her canvas away as she sat up, already grabbing at my coffee cup. "I have stuff I need to get done today besides this."

"I like it," I said, gesturing toward the painting. It was full of colors, separated by thick, hard lines, reminding me of a stained glass window. At the center of it was nothing but light, as darkness and shadows crinkled all around. "What is it?"

"A neo-expressionist supernova."

"You know, I was just going to guess that." I grinned. I didn't know much about art, but I knew how to tease her. "I think you've captured it perfectly."

From her expression, I knew Raiya could tell I was bantering. "Thanks, but it's far from done."

"Are you sure you want to stop?" I asked. "I know you like to do this stuff."

She shook her head, pushing her long hair back from her face as she sipped my coffee. "It's fine."

"Alright."

I watched as she put the rest of her supplies up, before she flopped down on her bed and reached for her shoes.

"What are you doing here?" She smirked. "Have you come to apologize, by any chance?"

"Not really," I said. "But I can fake one, if you'd like." I decided not to turn the tables on her by asking if she wanted to apologize to me. Her arrow might have pierced Draco, but it could've been a better shot. She would've defeated him, and we could have been on our merry way to a normal date night instead of worrying about SWORD and Draco's next moves.

She distracted me as she swirled the coffee around in the cup. "Stubborn." She sighed. "I should've guessed."

"I came to tell you about Martha," I said. "I got some information from her about SWORD."

"She told you about them?" Raiya's eyes sparked with instant surprise.

"Well, sort of. I was looking for information on Otherworld, Inc., the company Dante said he worked for, and she told me it's a new company. There's reason to believe it's a front."

"She told you this?"

"I asked her to help," I explained. "I thought it was a good idea—"

Raiya stopped me. "What?!"

"Come on. I told you she used to work for them. She told me that herself."

"Still, that doesn't mean that you have her go snooping around for us. It could be dangerous."

"I'd say it's more dangerous for them than it is for her," I remarked. "This is Martha, after all. She can be terrifying if she doesn't like you."

"But—"

"Just let me tell you what I know," I said, trying to hold in my irritation. *How many times is she going to interrupt me?*

"Fine." She folded her arms across her chest and looked at me expectantly.

"She told me that Otherworld was a new company, set up this year, and its mailing address is in the Time Tower, same as the Skarmastad Foundation."

"Is that it?"

"Well, she confirmed Dante's the lead on the project," I said.

"So Otherworld is a fake company," Raiya repeated, "and Dante is heading the situation here in the city? That's all?"

"That's all," I said.

"It's not that much," Raiya said.

"Hey, it's more than I've been able to find in the last several months, looking through Cheryl's files and scanning through the city payouts."

"It still doesn't seem worth it to ask Mrs. Smithe to risk her safety for."

"She agreed to it, didn't she? That's something," I argued. "Besides, now we know that Dante's leading up a smaller force here. We don't need to worry about SWORD so much."

"Just because Otherworld is a new and smaller company doesn't mean they don't have other forces stationed here," Raiya pointed out. "That's precisely why it should be a concern."

Anger washed over me, and I gave up trying to stay above its dark water. "It's hardly a concern when compared to your ancient grandfather-turned-immortal-dragon, especially since you can't take him down."

"You really want me to destroy my own grandfather?" Raiya asked.

"That's not a fair question," I said.

She shot up out of her seat. "You're not being fair, either!"

"I think it's still a legitimate question. We need to be able to make sure we can do our job."

"That's not our only concern," Raiya snapped back. "We have to make sure that the people we protect are okay, too. And that's why I'm angry about Mrs. Smithe helping us out!"

"It was her choice," I replied.

"Yes, but you can't live with some decisions!" Raiya shouted.

The door to her room squeaked open. We jumped back, stepping apart from each other.

It was Elysian.

He sighed as he saw us. "Oh, great," he said. "I've either arrived in the middle of one of your make-out sessions or you've been arguing."

Raiya's cheeks burned red, matching, I suspected, my own. "We were not making out," I grumbled.

"I was going to bet on that," he said, "given the volume of your discussion, but it's still fifty-fifty, knowing you two."

"What brings you here, Elysian?" Raiya asked. "Besides, of course, Rachel's baking?"

"Hey, Jason's getting pretty good, too." Elysian scoffed. "No one seemed to mind me taking his burnt cookies."

I glared at him. "You know, Cheryl's been getting onto me about my bills," I said. "That's partially your fault."

"It is not my fault, however, that you have a job and your mother still pays your credit card bills," Elysian replied. Before I could retaliate on a more physical level, he added, "What's the big deal? She can afford it, and it's not like you pay anything either."

"Just stop it," Raiya said, turning to me. "Rachel uses you as a test subject more often than not, and for Jason's stuff, too. Your tab here will always be manageable."

"I'd rather it be non-existent than manageable," I bit back.

"You just can't stop, can you?" She rolled her eyes at me. "You know, I've known you now for over a year, and you still do that. Don't you think that's a bit immature?"

"Not if I'm right!"

Elysian let out a loud roar before our conversation could devolve any further. "If you could stop for a moment, I have some news."

Raiya frowned. "Fine. But hurry up. I have somewhere to I need to be."

"Alright," Elysian agreed. "I was headed over here—"

"Where do you need to be today?" I asked. "Your GED's not until this weekend."

"I have an appointment," she muttered.

"Excuse me," Elysian called. "Hello? Big news, anyone?"

I gave up on Raiya; she was obviously still angry with me. "Fine. What is it?"

"Mikey's out of the hospital," Elysian said. "I saw him walking through Shoreside Park just now while I was on my way over here."

"You didn't stop him?" I asked.

"Why would I?" Elysian snorted. "He's your friend, not mine."

Raiya sighed and stood up. "Why don't you two go and talk to him?" she said. "See if you can find out why Dante discharged him."

I rolled my eyes. "Cheryl's deadline for the *Flying Angels* case expires soon. He probably got out because she's not going to get an extension, so he's safe from her."

"You should still go and check."

"Maybe I should," I said, "but that might put his safety at risk."

"Well, it's so good to see you're working on that maturity already, Humdinger," Raiya retorted. "I'll see you later."

She sidestepped me and waltzed through the door, determined not to say anything else.

I glanced over at Elysian, who was frowning. "She's got a point," he admitted.

"Shut up."

"See? You have a problem."

"You're going to have some problems, too, if you keep it up," I warned. "You're lucky I'm more concerned about Mikey now."

"So we're going to go see him?" Elysian asked.

"Yes. Right now."

"Aw, I was hoping for a cookie before we left."

I sighed. It was times like these that I missed Aleia. She had her soft spots, but she was good at getting us going.

No wonder Raiya thinks I have a maturity problem. Look who I'm hanging out with.

☼<u>7</u>☼

SWORD's Play

It didn't take Elysian and me long to spot Mikey. Shoreside Park was just across the street and down a bit from Rachel's.

"Mikey!" I called out to him, but he didn't seem to hear me. "Geez, you'd think after all that time he spent by himself he'd be glad to see his friends."

"Are you still his friend?" Elysian asked.

"Uh, well, I … I guess that's the question to ask," I admitted. "I haven't seen him since January."

"Nice," Elysian muttered.

"Hey, I've been busy," I reminded him. "The assistant mayor's a slave driver, school was still going on, I was studying for the SATs, and we all had to work on finding Draco."

"So tell me, how many times did you go to all-night gamer parties?"

The all-too-innocent look on his face made me frown. "Shut up."

"Come on, boss, don't be such a fascist," Elysian teased. "You need someone to keep you in line. That's why you have me. And that's why you argue with Starry Knight as often as you do."

"She's not always right," I insisted.

117

"It's better that you both keep each other in line, then," he said. "Personally, I don't think we would get along as well as we do if I had to do all the work by myself. It's too much work and you get too angry with people who try to correct you."

My fists clenched. "I hate you," I muttered under my breath.

"What did you say?"

"Nothing," I grunted. "Nothing that matters. We're here to see Mikey. That's what … " My voice trailed off as I realized I didn't know where he was.

I threw up my hands in exasperation. "Great! We lost him."

"You should've been paying better attention," Elysian told me.

I grabbed him by the scruff of his miniaturized dragon neck. "Are you kidding me?" I nearly screamed. "You were supposed to be paying attention, too!"

He jostled himself free of my grip. "There's no need to punish me for your problems. Go transform," he barked. "I'll take to the skies and search for him there."

I watched Elysian take off, before I grabbed my phone and called him. *There's no use doing something the hard way if you can avoid it.*

I only groaned when the call went right to voicemail. "I can't believe he doesn't have his phone on him," I muttered, before I ducked into a nearby wooded area.

Once I was out of sight, I pressed the mark on my wrist and felt the power blossom out inside of me. Energy charged through me, spurting out like lightning through my blood.

My wings fluttered wide open, and I took off. Flying with wings of fire never ceased to amaze me.

Up ahead of me, Elysian was spiraling in and out of the cloud cover, beckoning me to follow. "This way!" he called, before heading down to the ground.

I hurried to follow him, but I began to slow down when I finally caught sight of Mikey again.

He walked into the Time Tower.

Considering what I'd learned about Otherworld, and how the Skarmastad Foundation owned the building, I felt a distinct sense of reluctance as I stepped down onto the earth once more.

Elysian hovered beside me, slinking down to his smaller size. "Well?" he asked as he settled onto my shoulder.

"I don't know," I said. "I can't imagine why he would be here."

"Maybe he's meeting Dante," Elysian suggested.

"That makes sense," I said. "Okay. Let's go. If nothing else, we can see what Dante knows about Draco and his connection to the Skarmastad Foundation."

As we walked inside the building, I realized there weren't a lot of people around; hardly any passersby, hardly any people nearby at all.

It's the perfect set up for Dante to meet Mikey, I thought.

"Hello there, Wingdinger."

Speaking of which …

Dante stood, leaning casually against the far wall as he looked at me. His goatee had grown more, since the last time I saw him, I noticed.

"It's a pleasure to see you again," he intoned, and instantly I knew something was wrong.

"Boss," Elysian whispered. "This is—"

"Yep," I said. "A set up. For us."

"Where's Starry Knight?" Dante asked as more SWORD agents began to peel away from the shadows.

"She's got things to do," I said, uneasily. I was beginning to see why Raiya didn't trust them. Besides the whole "being captured" by them the first time we met thing, too. "What do you want?"

"It's not what I want," he said as he began to saunter over to us. "It's what Apollo City wants. Assistant Mayor Dunbrooke has given the D. A. a time limit, and we've been instructed to assist her in getting you to cooperate."

Dante glanced over his shoulder. "My son has been kind enough to help us in getting your attention."

"Mikey?" My gaze shot to him as I realized he'd been standing behind Dante.

Mikey stepped forward, hesitant but still determined.

What in the world is going on?!

"What did you do?" I whispered.

Mikey came and stood beside me. "Come on, give me a break. Grandpa Odd came to visit me in the hospital," he told me. "He said SWORD had reached out to you, that you could heal all the people with the sickness, including Gwen, but you weren't willing to help out."

"Oh, Mikey … " I could've cheerfully shot him. And myself. I was the one, after all, who did not visit him, and I didn't tell him about Grandpa Odd's true identity.

Elysian snorted, sending sparks flying. "This is Draco's game," he said, voicing my thoughts.

Mikey ignored him. "When Dad came to the hospital, I asked him about it. He said we could try to get you to cooperate if I helped out."

"They needed you. They used you!" I shook my head. "All that time in the hospital and you've gone soft-headed. They tricked you."

Mikey frowned. "I'm just trying to get people back to their normal lives," he said bitterly. "I know I would feel much better if Gwen was better."

"You're an idiot," I said. "You just gave up on life because you couldn't have things go your way?" I grabbed his arm, making Dante step forward menacingly. *Great. They've managed to bond over making me the bad guy.*

While I dropped Mikey's arm, I didn't stop glaring at him. "I told you I would take care of things on my own. Starry Knight and I are working on it. We're so close."

"Well, these guys can get you closer," Mikey said. "That's what Grandpa told me."

"He's not your real grandpa," I hissed. *"He's the enemy!"*

"Well, it's too late," he said. "Dad's here, and they need your help."

"Don't you know 'needing help' is code for—wait, what?" I sputtered. "Why did you call him 'Dad?' You don't even like him."

"He's the only one who came to visit me and didn't seem to think it was a chore," Mikey said. He shrugged, suddenly very uncomfortable. I didn't even have to read his emotions to see it. "Besides, he *is* my dad, after all."

Oh, great.

I closed my eyes, and it was just as well that I did. I barely saw Mikey get tasered, before I was tasered, and Elysian tried to fight off the other guards.

THE STARLIGHT CHRONICLES

☼

I woke up, probably hours later, groggy and grunting in pain. I was cold, and I was alone.

A rush of recognition and fear flooded through me. This had happened before, at SWORD's black site by the marina, where I was dragged off after I stopped Starry Knight's supernova.

Same as last time, I was still cold, and my wings were still able to cushion me from the hardwood floor. Not too many things were different this time around; I knew for certain I was in another location. Looking around at the near-empty office-like room I was in, I estimated I was in the Time Tower still.

At least last time, Raiya was with me.

Thinking of Raiya calmed me down.

I hated our fight earlier, but maybe it was good that we fought earlier, or she would have been captured, too.

She said she had somewhere she needed to be, but I was more than willing to bet Raiya made that up just so she didn't have to be around me. After I made her so upset, I could hardly blame her.

Looking around at the small, dark room I was trapped in, she would probably say that I was getting my comeuppance.

Mikey betrayed me, while SWORD captured me. Yep, that was some hardcore poetic justice.

And I didn't even know if they did anything else to me, I realized. *What if they put a monitoring chip in me? Or if they're running my prints? Or if they took DNA samples to compare to my records?*

All of the alien abduction shows I'd seen over the years came crashing into my mind, making one big pile-up of fear, panic, and madness. "Ugh," I groaned. They were going to find out who I was. If Mikey hadn't told them already.

My stomach rumbled. At least that was one question answered. I'd been stuck long enough I was hungry again.

Time passed slowly. It was worse than when I was stuck in the classroom for my SATs, but that might have been because I didn't have a clock to count the seconds. Of course, that might have made it go faster, too.

"You're killing me, Aleia," I muttered. "Or is this Alora's fault?"

"Blaming someone else for your problems? That's not going to help you." The door opened and a figure walked in. "It's no one's fault but your own that you're in this position."

I tensed up immediately at the sound of my mother's voice.

I'd had nightmares about this very situation. And here it was, coming to complete fruition. My mother, the talented lawyer, was here, and she was going to get the legal right to whip me.

"Where's Dante?" I asked.

Cheryl turned toward the door, where two SWORD agents appeared. "He's not your concern," she said. "You're dealing with me now."

I stood up (no need to look sloppy as I fell on the mercy of the court) and met Cheryl's gaze. She would appreciate the courage, I thought. There was nothing she could respect more than a worthy opponent, and I was determined to give her one as her offspring, even if she didn't know it.

Which brought me to my first goal: Establish what she knew, without giving away anything else. That was going to require a lot of bluffing.

"So," I said, "nice to meet you at last, formally."

Cheryl narrowed her gaze. She was going to try to break me by getting me to break me, I realized.

All I had to do was clam up. I knew I could outwait her.

Even if my stomach couldn't.

"Hungry?" she asked me as my stomach gurgled loudly.

"Just a little bit," I muttered apologetically.

"I can make arrangements."

"No thanks. I've seen that trick before."

"I can make other arrangements, if you're interested," Cheryl began. Her waiting had ended. She just wanted to get to a deal.

I remembered tonight was the deadline for her case. If I could hold out to midnight, she would have no legal right to keep me, since the assistant mayor had put an expiration on the case.

But that was only if I didn't give anything away, didn't admit to anything, and somehow managed to escape without giving her just cause to keep me for another felony.

That was going to be harder.

A small push behind my heart comforted me. *Raiya is not here. We are both required to be here for any case to proceed.*

Immediately I relaxed—slightly. No need to tip Cheryl off.

Ah, who could be immune to the rush of pleasure after realizing such profound logic, provided so divinely?

"I'm not interested in making arrangements right now," I assured Cheryl.

"Why not?" Cheryl asked. "You and your friends are facing massive fines, possible prison time, not to mention the more unpleasant task of facing the press."

"I've got a distinct advantage when it comes to dodging them," I said, indicating my wings.

Cheryl frowned. "There's no way you can run from the law."

"I happen to know the law says that you don't have much longer for your case to proceed," I said. "So it's not a matter of 'where,' so much as 'when.'"

"Dante was right," she growled. "You're a troublemaker."

"I'm a troublemaker who he is protecting," I said.

"It's easier to do that from a prison cell with round-the-clock surveillance," Cheryl shot back.

I tried not to let the truth of that bother me. I shrugged. "I imagine you might think so," I said.

Why was it so hard to be cool, like in the movies? But then, I supposed, I'd only been captured a few times. I needed to get more experience in before I judged my performance too harshly.

"That's all you have to say for yourself?" Cheryl asked. "After the lives you've destroyed, all the damage you've caused, and all the trouble you've brought to the city?"

"Yep."

Cheryl put her hands on her hips. She was prepared to do battle. "You seem pretty confident," she said, trying to wheedle me. She was going the route of circumvention, it looked like.

"I'm a teenager," I said. "I'm good at faking it."

"And you've done this before? You've gotten in trouble with the law?"

"I have been accused of breaking the law," I said. "It doesn't mean that I actually broke the law."

"Semantics," Cheryl assured me. "A jury doesn't want the truth; they just want to hear a good story."

"Narrative fallacy is common enough," I told her. "And it's easily debunked with the truth."

"There is no such thing as 'truth,' in this case," Cheryl countered. "It's only a matter of perspective."

"If there's no such thing as objective truth," I said, "then there wouldn't be a law for me to break, would there?"

She seemed taken aback. For a moment, I imagined my mother, a woman who would could give mannequins lessons in looking perfect, fluster as I easily parried her attacks.

"You think you're clever," she muttered, pacing the room in front of me. "Or you have a reason to believe nothing is going to happen to you. Tell me why."

"Why?" I couldn't resist teasing her. This was the most mother-son bonding we'd done in years.

"Because I'm interested. What's the point in being brilliant if you don't have an appreciative audience?"

"Is that why you want to prosecute me?" I asked. *That* seemed to make sense. There was no denying that Cheryl was very ambitious. Even the rest of her relatives, the little I knew of my extended family, knew not to get in her way.

With me, she'd always pushed me to get my law degree, get some practice in, and then run for public office. Maybe she was hoping, with her special D. A. appointment, she might get further assignment higher up one day, too.

It wouldn't surprise me.

"We're not here because of me," Cheryl countered. "We're here—"

"Because the city needs a scapegoat and you want to further your career." I snorted. "That's all."

"You've been accused of disturbing the peace, for damages—"

"I've heard of it," I said, silently reminding myself at the last moment not to let it slip that I helped write it. "And I know for a fact that Starry Knight is also listed on the lawsuit. You can't file it without both of us present."

"You're not willing to renegotiate terms?" Cheryl asked. "We could drop the charges against her if you wanted to take full responsibility."

I clenched my fists. "No," I said. "Starry Knight and I are in this together."

"You'd have her tried and sentenced alongside you?"

"We're allies."

"And lovers?"

My face felt hot all of a sudden. "We're together," I murmured, hoping that was enough to get her to leave that part of it alone. Superhero or not, I couldn't imagine any teenager willingly having the sex talk with his or her parents. Or his butler.

"I saw that kid's blog out there," Cheryl told me. "He seems to think that you'll confess, especially if it's to protect her."

"I suppose he was the one who told you who I am?" I asked. *This is it! The moment of truth …*

I held my breath nervously.

"He said he could get you here." Cheryl tapped her foot against the floor. "He was right about that."

"He was expecting Starry Knight, too, wasn't he?" I almost laughed. "She's busy today."

"Hopefully she's not too busy," Cheryl said. "In the event that we are unable to come to an acceptable agreement here today, Otherworld, Inc. will be taking you into their full custody."

"That's fine with me," I said. "Their mission is to protect me."

Cheryl laughed, making me feel uncomfortable. "That might be part of it," she said. "But they have other plans as well. They've assured me they have a great many cases on which they could use your help."

Swallowing suddenly seemed beyond my capabilities. I thought about what Martha had told me before: SWORD would find a way to use people if they need cooperation. They weren't above murder or torture if they needed it.

And, I had to uncomfortably admit, they might be tempted to see me as another agent, like Dante, if they had the right amount of leverage.

I decided the next time I talked to Dante, I would beat him up.

SWORD was in the business of power—power for themselves first.

This has to be why Raiya's against them. They want to use us to save the world from threats like Alküzor and Draco, and then they want us to work for them.

They would likely be able to make us, too. Martha had been discharged, but not before she paid a hefty price.

What about Dante? I wondered. *Was it possible he'd been coerced into service, too?*

That would possibly explain his soft spot for Mikey. Of course, Mikey was actually his son.

"What do you know about Otherworld?" I asked. "Do you know they're a front company for a shadow organization?"

"That sounds like a movie," Cheryl said dismissively. "Weren't you the one that was just trying to point out the shortcomings of narrative fallacy?"

"It's true." I pushed forward. "They're a front for an organization known as SWORD."

"SWORD?"

"The, er, Special World Organization and Research Division," I said, hoping that I remembered it correctly (stupid acronyms.)

Cheryl cocked her eyebrow at me. "That's the best you've got?"

Before I could answer, there was a resounding *bang!* from behind the door.

I could feel the heat of Elysian's familiar fire, and I could hear Starry Knight calling out orders as they burst into the building.

I grinned as I saw familiar flickers of light casting new shadows underneath the door. The SWORD agents guarding us ran out of the room to help, and I grinned as I glanced back at Cheryl.

"No," I said, "*she's* the best I've got."

Cheryl muttered a string of curses as she followed the guards out the door.

Before I could escape her, she turned to me. "You stay here. You're in custody; as long as you cooperate, you'll be safe. But if you put so much as a finger out this door, we'll have no choice but to take action."

"I'm getting used to being tasered," I told her.

"I'll take that to mean you need more practice with it," Dante said. I realized he must have been waiting outside the door as I met with Cheryl.

Figures. He has to do to the whole creepy-stalker-spy thing.

"I'd hate to take up your time." I shuffled back a few steps regardless.

"Maybe Starry Knight will give me the pleasure," Dante said, pulling the weapon out of his coat pocket.

"You leave her out of this," I warned.

"We'll see." He smirked, probably cheering at the thought that he'd managed to get me riled. He would be that petty.

More calls came from outside the room. As Cheryl ran out the door, Dante stepped inside.

"Watch him," she ordered as she pushed past him.

Then I was left all alone with Dante.

It didn't take me long to start taunting him. "I see you've let Mikey out of his cage," I said.

"He called me himself," Dante replied. "He'd seen reason. He told me the truth." He pulled out a file from his pocket and unfolded it. "I'm guessing your mother doesn't know the truth, Hamilton?"

"If you didn't tell her," I said.

"I thought I would leave that up to you," Dante remarked. "After all, you're a star, aren't you? Figuratively speaking, I mean." The leer on his face tipped me off; he was trying to be funny, and it wasn't working.

He continued on when I said nothing. "Star of the swim team, top of the class, a favorite on the 'Hot List' of your high school elite, even Martha Smithe's favorite student. How quaint. I suppose you're the reason she came snooping around last week?"

Still, I said nothing.

Dante grinned. "You'll have to pardon me. As the son of Cheryl, the city's top lawyer, and Mark, my old best friend from high school, your tragedy is quite amusing to me."

"Because I was under your nose the entire time?" I asked, folding my arms across my chest. "Or because you gave away information to me without a second thought? Or," I continued, "is it because I was the one who helped Mikey go through losing his father when we were younger?"

From the expression on his face, stone silence wrapped in anger, I knew I'd hit a mark—and it stung.

"Leave him out of this," Dante hissed.

"He seems to have implicated himself already," I retorted. "Especially if he told you about me."

"He said you were smart."

"He wasn't lying."

"No, he wasn't," Dante agreed, and despite the fact he was my enemy at the moment, I felt a rush of pride. "He also told me that Starry Knight is your greatest weakness. He said you were in love with her."

"Love is not a weakness," I insisted.

"We have yet to see it as a strength."

"You told me before that you're here to protect me," I said, changing the topic. I didn't like it when he started talking about Starry Knight.

"And to do that," Dante grumbled, "we need your cooperation."

"Why are you helping my mother then?" I asked. "She'll destroy me in court."

"We have to cooperate with the city as well," he said. "We've made deals with the media and we've kept up a façade of comradery with the city. Part of that includes helping Cheryl."

"So you're not just sucking up to Cheryl and Mark?"

"No," Dante snapped.

I thought about it. Dante made me angry a lot, but he genuinely seemed concerned about Mikey, who, up until he brought me to the Time Tower, was a friend of mine. He also seemed to actually like Mark and, if nothing else, tolerate Cheryl. Maybe I could use that as a bargaining chip of sorts, to keep Raiya's involvement to a minimum.

Before I could put forth some kind of proposal, there was a beeping noise.

Dante glanced down at his watch, and I noticed that there was only silence from the other side of the room.

While he was busy, I turned and burst the door open.

Only to see Starry Knight, followed closely by Cheryl, heading toward me.

"Starry Knight," I called, excited to see her.

There was a rush of relief that radiated from inside her, one that nearly bowled me over. On the outside, she looked bored and resolute.

I had a lot to learn from Starry Knight, especially when it came to self-control.

Dante grabbed me from behind, firmly holding onto my arm. "We have a meeting arranged in here," he said. He glanced down at me. "Starry Knight has promised to surrender."

"What?!" I balked at the very thought of her at the mercy of my mother. It was nothing short of ironic to me that I was born as the Star of Mercy, because I knew Cheryl had exactly none—especially when it came to her court cases.

"Come inside," Cheryl instructed me and Starry Knight, as she gestured to Dante. He dropped me before heading over to a closet. From the shadows, two chairs suddenly appeared.

"What were you thinking?" I muttered to Raiya as she reached out and put a hand on my arm. "This is *Cheryl* we're dealing with."

"I'm happy to see you, too," she said, her voice hushed. "Do you realize you've been missing for a whole day?"

"No." I struggled to reorient myself to the time. It was strange that it was lost, even though seconds before I hadn't missed it.

"I could feel your pain." I noticed for the first time her hands were shaking slightly as she held onto me.

"What do you mean?" I asked. "I wasn't in any pain." *Not that I could remember, anyway.* "Did you think Draco had gotten to me?"

Raiya ignored my question. "I was worried for you."

"I'm worried for you now," I whispered back.

"I'm the one with the plan right now," she said, giving me a small shadow of a smile, one I could barely see in the dim light.

"Stop muttering to yourselves and sit down," Cheryl barked. "We have business to discuss."

Raiya moved swiftly around me. "Indeed we do, Mrs. Dinger," she agreed. "You said this meeting would be in complete privacy."

"Dante here is an agent assigned to protect me and support my mission to bring you to justice," Cheryl replied. "He is an extension of myself. I will not send him away."

Raiya frowned at Dante, and then glanced back at me. That was obviously not part of her plan, I realized.

Come to think of it, I mused, Mikey had told Dante who *I* was. There'd been no indication Mikey had revealed Starry Knight's true identity.

Only a handful of people knew Raiya and I were dating—including Mikey and Cheryl. But—but—it was possible that she could get out of this without revealing herself to SWORD.

"Fine," Raiya said, interrupting my thoughts.

"No, it's not," I said, jumping up. SWORD already knew who I was. Or at least, Dante did. There was no way to be sure of everything, including if they knew Raiya and I were together, but if there was a chance I could save her from being entangled in their operations, I had to take it.

Cheryl instantly rebounded on me. "Starry Knight is here because she agreed to surrender," she said. "In exchange, we have agreed that you will not be harmed."

"I won't have her harmed in my place," I objected.

"No one said anything about harming people," Cheryl insisted. "This is a matter of breaking the law."

"We haven't broken any laws," I argued. "And I would know that better than anyone. Even you, Cheryl … or should I saw 'Mom?'"

"Hamilton, you're supposed to call me … "

That was the moment when I should've had the camera ready. Once more, the opportunity passed and I was unable to take it. My mother, always precise and proper, slumped over as her mouth dropped open.

Cheryl sank into silence, before she looked over at Dante, who nodded.

"I see … " she murmured. She turned her attention down to her phone, where she fiddled with it long enough to convince me she was struggling to find a way to respond, and short enough to convince me she was at a loss.

Probably for the first time in *years*, she was at a loss.

I took Raiya's hand, lacing my fingers through hers. I was desperately hoping that Cheryl would get the message and not reveal Raiya as Starry Knight.

Secrets upon secrets, I thought with a silent groan.

"I know that you promised someone once," I said, "that if there was a time when you were able to help, you would give it."

"What are you … ?" Cheryl's voice trailed off as I tugged harder on Raiya's hand. She glanced from me to Raiya, and then back again. From her expression, I knew my plan was working; I knew she was thinking of her promise to Raiya.

She was picturing that moment in the hospital, at Adam's birth, when, after nearly losing him, he was handed back to her, his health restored thanks to Raiya's blood donation. Her emotions all corresponded to such an event; desperation, panic, the most primal sort of terror, and helplessness—all of

THE STARLIGHT CHRONICLES

this, before the innocent pure euphoria of something deeper than relief.

As desperate as she had once been, I found myself now.

"If you need more proof," I said quietly, "I can transform back into my normal self."

"No, that won't be necessary," Cheryl replied instantly. I think she was afraid to face the truth.

I tried to smile for her. "This should explain some of my missed curfews better," I said.

"Dante," Cheryl snapped. "Leave us."

His eyebrows raised in surprised. "Are you sure?" he asked.

"Yes. Leave."

Dante's lips tightened, but he followed orders.

The instant the door shut behind him, Cheryl stood up. "I knew you were dangerous," she said, snapping at Raiya.

"Anyone who manages to get you to owe them a favor is dangerous." I snorted. I pushed myself out in front of Raiya, protecting her from my mother's wrath.

Non-ironically, Cheryl's expression did remind me of Taygetay at the moment, as she fumed in pacing steps around the room.

"How could you do this?" she asked, turning her attention to me. "All this, *and* you attacked your father and brother in the hospital a few weeks ago?"

"Some of the reports were greatly exaggerated," I said. "You can talk to Mark about it later."

"Mrs. Dinger," Raiya spoke up. "I'm going to ask—"

"No!" Cheryl interrupted. "Don't say it. Don't ask that of me."

Raiya frowned. "Your son's future is on the line," she pointed out. "There is no cause on which we should agree more."

"My son has lied to me," Cheryl argued. "And he's been breaking the rules by seeing you."

"I offered to trade myself in for him," Raiya reminded her, "and I would like to make good on—"

"Hey, stop right there," I interrupted. "You're not doing that for me."

I stepped in front of her. "If you don't drop the case against her, I'll go public. I'll humiliate the family name, and I'll lose out on going to college and the presidency and every other good thing you've ever thought I would achieve."

"You don't know what you're saying," Cheryl grumbled.

"No, you're wrong. I know exactly what I'm saying," I said. I turned to Raiya, who had a surprised look on her face. I gripped her hand again.

Raiya's resolve came back at my determination. "I'm sure if anyone can find a way to throw out this case, it's you, Mrs. Dinger."

Yes! I cheered to myself. Raiya was no longer protecting me; she was fighting for us.

"Adam's life is more than worth it," I added quietly.

"I was under a lot of stress when I made that promise," Cheryl muttered.

"Come on, Mom, seriously?" I frowned at her. "That excuse hardly gives you grounds to dismiss it."

"I also promised to uphold my duty the day I was given the job of District Attorney," Cheryl shot back. "Don't you dare lecture me on duty, Hamilton."

Raiya tightened her hold on me before I could respond, silently letting me know to wait it out. In the end, I think her way was better. As silent moments passed, Cheryl only became more agitated.

At last, Cheryl spoke. "Fine." She shook her head and sat down, placing her hand on her head in frustration. "Fine."

She picked up her phone again. This time, she punched in a number and waited for a response.

It came. "Hello? Carly? I need you to cancel my press conference and reschedule it for tomorrow morning."

She paused while the girl on the other end seemed to ask questions, and I exchanged glances with Raiya.

Cheryl really can be incredulous sometimes. I can't believe she actually booked a press conference!

"Yes, yes, they got away," Cheryl said, her teeth gritted together. Her voice was strained and her eyes were hard as she looked over at us. "Yes, I know the statute of limitations is up as of midnight tonight."

A moment later, she barked, "I can't do anything else about it. We'll have to spin it to make it look like the assistant mayor's fault, or something to that effect … "

I watched as she turned away and began pacing on the far side of the room.

"Geez," I muttered. "That's my mother for you," I whispered to Raiya.

"You didn't have to do that for me," she whispered back. "I could have made a deal with her to take away your charges."

"I know Cheryl is upset," I replied, "but she'll get over it. This is the first case in a while that's given her national coverage. When she calms down, she'll realize it was a pipe dream to begin with."

"Still—"

"Still nothing." I brought her hand up to my cheek. "We're in this together, right?"

Raiya smiled. "Yes, we are."

There was nothing in that moment that I wanted to do more than kiss her. But, given my mother was already unhappy, I decided to hold off for the moment.

"That reminds me," Raiya said. "I should probably go signal Elysian."

"What's he doing?"

"He's the one who managed to hold off a lot of the SWORD agents, or Otherworld officers," Raiya explained. "He's still out there, keeping the place at a standstill."

"Oh, good," I said. "I'm surprised he's not in here. He would've liked the chance to see me squirm."

"He might've liked it, but that wasn't going to happen while I was around," Raiya assured me. "Elysian knows that."

"Technically, one never knows when it comes to Cheryl," I said, gesturing back toward my angry mother.

I turned back just in time to see her hang up the phone. She gripped it hard; even in the low lighting, I could see her knuckles turning white.

"There," she said, facing us. "It's done. As of midnight tonight, you're free."

"Thank you," Raiya replied.

"Don't thank me," Cheryl scoffed. "But we're even now. I don't want to hear I owe you anything ever again."

"Done."

Cheryl turned to me. "And you … you! I can't believe it. My own son has turned against me."

"I'm not against you," I said. "I've never been against you."

"Really?" Cheryl turned and narrowed her eyes at Raiya. "I can think of a few good examples."

"If you keep that up," I said, "you're going to make me change my mind."

Softening my expression, I came up to her. "You are my mother," I said. "You know me. You know we have our shortcomings and our spats, but I wouldn't try to hurt you more than staying out and breaking curfew to spite you."

Cheryl shook her head. "That's enough," she said. "Your father and I will discuss this later."

I decided not to tell her that he knew the truth, too. That was something she should hear from Mark himself, I knew.

Cheryl brushed past me, ignoring Raiya completely as she opened the door and walked out.

I saw Dante's shadow move in on her, and felt his confusion as he realized the truth of what happened.

Well, more or less the truth. He didn't need to know the exact details of the truth. I knew I could count on Cheryl to keep quiet, too—if she was the one person who could've broken Mikey, she was also the one person who wouldn't be broken.

Speaking of Mikey …

I turned back to Raiya. "Let's go," I said.

"Where?" she asked.

THE STARLIGHT CHRONICLES

"We need to find Mikey," I said. "I was captured because I saw him walking here."

"He brought you to them?"

"Yes," I admitted, feeling stupid about it now. "He told me that he revealed to Dante who I was—"

"So they do know for sure who you are?" Raiya asked. The worried tone of her voice made me falter slightly.

"It doesn't matter," I insisted, hoping that was the truth. "They don't know about you, or that we're dating." *I hope.*

"I'm not worried for me," Raiya told me. "I can fight off SWORD."

I thought about what Martha had said, about how we were up against a cunning opponent when it came to SWORD. "I don't think that will matter so much," I said, "especially if we can get to Mikey."

"But he was the one who told them about us."

"Exactly," I said. "They failed to get us to court. He just turned us in, and now we're free. He's going to have to find some way to be cooperative."

"I see what you mean," Raiya said, "even if I don't agree with your conclusions."

"About which part?" I asked. "The part where we can get Mikey to cooperate, or the part where it doesn't matter if SWORD knows who I am?"

"Both." She sighed. "But if he's here, we should get him. Come on, Elysian is waiting for us, too."

"Wait." I took her arm and drew her close to me.

All the worry in the world would wait while I kissed her. The instant her soft lips were pressed against mine, everything seemed to right itself. I was caught up in an everlasting moment, a moment where time had no measure, beauty had no end, and truth had no competition. I felt her pleasure, and knew it as my own as it radiated between us.

The world could be falling apart, I thought, *and as long as I had her beside me, I would welcome it.*

I drew back from her reluctantly, the taste of her still tingling on my lips. "There," I said, tugging her toward the door. "Now we can go."

147

☼8☼
Friends and Family

Finding Mikey—or rather, not finding Mikey—quickly made me worried.

I was briefly able to remember he'd been tasered along with me, and I feared for him once Raiya, Elysian, and I were all able to escape the Time Tower and we weren't able to find him.

A large part of me was still upset about his betrayal, and another part of me, a very, very, very small part, said that Draco was most likely behind it.

And that was the part that made me worry.

Draco vowed before he would frustrate us as we attempted to stop him. While Mikey should've known better, and I should've told him about Grandpa Odd's true identity, and I should've tried harder to visit him in the hospital …

You know what? I'm going to stop that train of thought right there.

After hours of searching, I stared up at the sky as I was standing on the edge of the boardwalk by Lake Erie. My wings drifted softly along with the light, springtime breeze.

Even from where I was standing, I could see the Time Tower, like a great white sword, sticking up from the ground, piercing the bodies and souls of mankind as easily as it stabbed the city cloud cover.

Raiya landed beside me on the docks of the marina. "He's not over at the observatory," she said.

Elysian came up to us a moment later, his tail whipping through the wind. "No luck in the downtown area by the college," he reported.

"It's entirely possible he's moving around," Raiya reminded us. She clenched her hands into fists. "It's times like this when I miss Aleia."

"Not that you don't miss her anyway," I said.

Raiya nodded. "You're right. It was very nice to see her down here."

Elysian shuffled his claw against the wooden landing. "It's getting late," he said. "We're not going to find him while you two have a pity party."

"First of all," I said, "if we were having any kind of party, we wouldn't be inviting you. Second, we're doing about all we can right now."

"Did you try calling him?" Raiya asked, while Elysian stuck his long tongue out at me.

"Yes," I said. I held up my phone. "He hasn't answered his phone in weeks though. I wondered if his mom stopped paying on it."

"Well, we've searched through all of the likely places in the city," Raiya said. She counted off her fingers as she listed them. "We checked his house, the school, the marina, the college, some hotels, and Rachel's."

"Do you think he was still in the Time Tower when we left?" I asked.

We all looked at each other, and we all knew what we were thinking: No one really wanted to go back there. Not tonight, anyway.

"Well, I have school tomorrow," I said. "I'd better get back. Cheryl's got more reasons now than ever to chide me for slipping up."

"Be careful," Raiya said. "I know she's your mother, but I don't want you to let your guard down."

"I won't." I turned to Elysian. "I've got backup, besides."

She smiled, and then reached over and pet Elysian on the head. "That's true. I do count on you to take care of him, Elysian."

Elysian puffed. "Someone's got to do it."

"Yeah," I said, "and I do it just fine, thank you very much."

Raiya gave me a quick kiss on the cheek. "Good night," she said. "I'll be working the early shift tomorrow at Rachel's if you come by in the morning."

"What do you mean, 'if?'" I asked, playfully twirling a lock of her hair in my fingers.

"You didn't come this morning. Well, yesterday morning, but this time."

"Because I was apparently kidnapped."

"That's why I got worried," she said.

"Elysian was with me. Why didn't he tell you where I was?"

"They managed to hold me down for a bit," Elysian admitted. "And when I got free, I ran into Draco."

"You did?" Raiya and I turned on him at the same time.

"Yes." Elysian shrugged, sending a ripple down his long body. "He was close by, enjoying the scene."

"Did he see you? Did you talk to him?" Raiya asked.

"Yes, to both questions," Elysian grumbled. He raised his left wing. "And more, too."

"Ugh." I nearly puked at the sight of the wound under his wing. There was a purplish-green x-shaped gash, bubbling over with a thin layer of translucent scales.

"Are you alright?" Raiya rushed forward, but Elysian reared back.

"Don't," he said. "Don't. Dragon's blood is powerful; it could hurt you."

"It's me," Raiya said. "I don't have healing powers for nothing."

"Nothing's all that you're going to be able to do for me," he snapped. "You're a Star, and a Starlight Warrior, a defender of the earth. I'm not part of that world."

"But you're part of ours," Raiya insisted.

For a moment, Elysian's eyes glazed over. He finally shook his head. "No," he said. "No, I'm not."

He shuffled his tail and turned, clearly hurting Raiya.

Before he could go, I said, "Don't worry about it, Starry Knight. He always thought he was better than us."

Elysian flicked his tail back at me, sending me flying into the water of the marina.

I grappled with the water, surprised to see my wings still on fire, even as I pushed myself back to the other side of the water.

When I resurfaced, it was just in time to see Elysian as he took off.

Raiya reached down and grabbed me. "Are you okay?" she asked, pulling on my hand as she dragged me back from the chill of the night waters.

"I'm fine," I told her, spitting out my disgust as well as some of the lake water.

"You didn't have to insult him, you know," Raiya told me as she finished freeing me from the lake. "My feelings can take a hit."

"He was hurting me, too," I said. "And while he spoke the truth, I did, too."

"I know you and Elysian have always had a bit of a rough relationship," she said gently.

"You have a gift for understating things," I told her, pushing the wet wingdings out of my eyes. "But I'd rather talk about your other gifts right now."

She shot me a confused, suspicious look. "I'm not going to kiss you right now," she said, "even if you're pretending you were dashing and charming tonight."

"Not that gift," I said. "I meant your coffee-making skills."

"I thought you had school tomorrow?"

"But I get to be with you tonight," I said. "Throw some coffee in, and I'll be more than fine."

She pursed her lips together in thoughtful consideration.

It is time to give in, I thought. "Please, Raiya? Don't make me go home to Cheryl and Elysian. Not without proper sustenance."

Raiya grinned. "I suppose Rachel's is open for a bit longer."

"Exactly."

It turned out to be the best thing ever, to go and hang out with Raiya for a bit after searching for Mikey.

True, we could've continued the search, but I was cold and wet, courtesy of Elysian, and I considered Rachel's a place for healing as well as comfort.

He was lucky I didn't get pneumonia.

But those weren't the only reasons it was the best thing ever to be with Raiya. I mean on top of the normal reasons, too, like how I loved her and I loved being with her and how I loved the smell of the special espresso beans Rachel ordered.

It was the best thing ever hanging out with her, because I woke up to approximately the worse thing ever.

My mother had me woken up at the crack of dawn the next day so I could head down to City Hall and help her with her new press conference talking points.

As I ran around the small auditorium at City Hall, taking orders for coffee, getting supplies, and helping with the lighting, I almost wondered if Cheryl was doing this in order to punish me. I wondered if she was going to rat me out anyway.

After a few moments and a few sips of Rachel's coffee Mayor Mills had the brilliance to stock, I figured that was as crazy as it was unlikely.

Why would she reveal my identity now, when she could hold it over my head for several years to come?

That was the Cheryl I knew.

THE STARLIGHT CHRONICLES

As the news media shuffled in, minus a few of its more familiar faces, Cheryl came up beside me.

"Are you ready?" I asked her.

"No."

My eyes widened briefly at her admission. "Are you afraid?"

"It's not a matter of fear," she said, "but rather what you are afraid of, Hamilton."

"So, yes?" I guessed.

She frowned at me. "We're here because of you and your girlfriend, remember?"

"You leave her out of this," I warned. "She hasn't done anything wrong. Or illegal," I added, as Cheryl planted her hands on her hips.

"Fine," Cheryl remarked. She sighed. "I have tried to be a good mother, you know."

"You are a good mother," I told her. When she looked at me, surprised, I shrugged. "You're a good mother," I said, "but I think you're a better lawyer."

I was expecting her to frown again, but she smiled. "Well, that's good to hear, at least."

Why would that be a good *thing to hear?* I shook my head as my mother's name was called, and she went out to her adoring public.

I watched as the people began clapping and cheering when she walked out to the news podium. As much as I knew she was angry at me, and likely sad at her circumstances, I was proud of her. No one likes to lose, but there were a lot of people who wouldn't have been one-tenth as graceful as my mother over it.

My mother was a favorite among the crowds. As fearsome as she was in court, she was a compelling figure, and, for her age, even attractive. I could see why the public loved her and painted her out to be a true heroine among the many city prosecutors. Her ambition only endeared her more to the public.

Because, of course, the public didn't see her as I did, though in truth, they probably saw her more often than I did.

"Thank you, thank you very much," Cheryl began, smiling to the crowd.

I sighed as she talked for a bit about her many accomplishments, under the guise of thanking her public fans for all their support and votes since Stefano had taken office and used his influence to get her promoted.

Realization hit me hard and fast. *No wonder Cheryl's been so focused on this case. She's trying to run for re-election.*

I knew before her initial appointment was special, because the last mayor of Apollo City had been forced to resign, and several workers with the city, unwilling or unable to handle the supernatural crises, had stepped down as well, citing irreconcilable differences with the change in leadership.

Cheryl had followed Stefano's lead in prosecuting the superheroes because it translated into votes. She wanted to run for the office on her own terms.

I was cynical enough to wonder how she was going to present this case to the public, so they would see she had no choice but to call it off.

"So, let's get down to business," Cheryl said, and the crowd went wild, interrupting the last of my thoughts. "We are unable to continue any further with the *Flying Angels* case. Assistant Mayor Dunbrooke, who has stepped up to fill in the gaping hole left by the estimable Mayor Mills while he is recovering from his heart attack—"

It was hard not to gag or laugh while she managed to compliment and insult both leaders simultaneously.

Only my mother. I shook my head, even as I admired her for her skill.

There were some questions that followed, but Cheryl never faltered.

"Mrs. Thomas-Dinger," one called out. "What will you be focused on now that the case has been called off?"

"Thank you for your question," Cheryl said. "I have decided to step down from my position as District Attorney."

A collective gasp went through everyone, including me.

"What? Why?" I stammered.

Fortunately, someone else with a mic asked the same question (different tone.)

"I have been practicing law for over a decade now," Cheryl said. "I've had several victories, and some losses."

There were cheers and one collective "Aw" from the crowd.

"While I work hard at what I do," Cheryl continued, "I feel I have reached my potential in serving the city. I wish to redirect my efforts into other areas of my life, not the least of which is being a mother to my two sons."

She could've gotten in her car, run me over, backed up and run me over three more times, and I would've been less shocked than I was at her admission.

More questions came, and minutes passed. Cheryl thanked the crowd, told them she would continue to work hard and lead a good life, and then she exited the stage. More reporters tried to follow her, asking her other questions, but she simply waved them off.

She came back up and stood beside me. "Well?" she asked. "How was that?"

"Astonishing," I said. It was the only word I could think of. "I think I'm dreaming."

"You're not," Cheryl snapped.

"Have you talked about this with Dad?" I asked.

"Since when do you care about what your father thinks?" Cheryl shook her head. "I have worked in law for a long time, Hamilton. No vacations unless they were mandated, no time off for being sick, and no rest taken unless pills were involved. I have made enemies of different people, people who have been put away, and others who are awaiting probation."

"So?" I asked. "You've done well."

"Thank you," she said. "But you said it yourself. I'm a good mother, but a better lawyer. I've perfected my lawyering. Now I can work on the mothering."

That was heartfelt and disconcerting all at the same time.

"With Adam, I hope," I said. "You might as well consider me a lost cause."

"I don't think so, not quite yet," she said. "But you'll get there, don't worry."

I'm pretty sure she was teasing me, but after all the shock I'd received from her already, I was done. "I'm leaving," I said, turning away. "I got to go to school."

"Don't forget to stop for coffee on the way," Cheryl called.

I stopped in my tracks. Glancing back, I eyed her carefully. "Does this mean you're okay with Raiya now?"

"If I am, are you more likely to dump her?"

I grinned, despite myself. "No."

"Then it doesn't matter, does it?" She waved. "Now, I've got to go home and settle into a week-long vacation before I set up my own law firm."

I laughed as I headed out.

Of course, Cheryl will never be down for long.

But seeing her give up her dreams humbled me. As much as I didn't want to care about it, I knew she was giving up something precious for me. That took more than love and unselfishness—that took a special kind of courage.

Raiya met me as I walked down the street toward Rachel's.

"How did you know I was coming?" I asked her as she handed me a large cup of my favorite mocha.

"I saw the press conference," she explained. "You know Rachel has the news on all the time. It's been exploding across the front page, about your mother."

"She's always been flashy about headlines," I murmured, taking a drink.

"You look nice in your dress clothes," Raiya said.

"I don't have time to change before going to school."

"Then don't go."

"Huh?" I glanced at her, surprised. Usually it was Elysian who was trying to convince me that school didn't matter so long as I had demons to destroy, and even then, I was already doing so well that a day off wouldn't hurt me at all.

"I said, don't go," she repeated.

"Why would I do that?"

"I found Mikey," she said. "He's back at the hospital. Just for a bit," she said, noting my concerned look.

"How do you know that's where he's at?"

"Your dad called and told me."

I frowned. "Okay, I feel like I am asking a lot of questions here, but why would my dad call and tell you that?"

"The day you were captured, I had to go to one of my doctor's appointments." She pointed to her heart, as if I were in second grade and didn't know where it was. "Dr. Dinger was scheduled to see me. So I went and I talked with him, and then I left."

"You didn't see Mikey there then," I said. "I was following him to the Time Tower."

"Your dad was calling me to see if I would reconsider," she said.

"Reconsider what?"

"I've decided to stop giving blood for now," she admitted. "When Grandpa—I mean, Draco—started taking me to the hospital, I don't think anyone was fully aware of my power. When your dad recognized it, he made sure I found out soon enough."

"So you did know, from pretty early on."

"Sure," she said. "It wasn't a hard guess, especially after I came into my powers. Your dad allowed me to help his research in a lot of ways."

"So I guess Adam's not the only one who's been helped by you."

Raiya nodded. "Anyway, I told him the other day I didn't want to come in and give blood anymore. There are too many confusing things between what Draco told me and what I think about it. I can always change my mind," she added quickly, "especially if there is a need for a special treatment or something."

"I'm glad you decided to stop," I said, reaching out and pulling her against me as we walked.

Tension broke around her and through her. It was strong enough I could sense it; I didn't even have to focus my power to see it. Her hands gripped me around my waist. "Me, too," she admitted quietly.

"How did my dad respond to that?" I asked. "Hopefully, it was better than how my mom took the news she wasn't going to be able to charge us."

"He was nice about it, even if he was disappointed." Raiya shrugged. "He said my heart does have some irregularities, and it would be good to still come in to get it checked. But I told him no."

"Why?"

"Because I can't do it without feeling terrible now. Even if I am helping him with his research or finding cures, I wouldn't feel right about it. You start to feel more like a test subject than a human after a while."

I considered this, and eventually agreed with her.

"I was thinking," Raiya said, "that rather than be a test subject, maybe it would be a good thing for me to still work with it. Become a doctor or nurse or something, you know?"

My head snapped around to face her.

"After all," she said with a grin, "we're going to need jobs once all this superhero business is over, right?"

At her words, I couldn't stop myself from kissing her.

"Hamilton." She gasped as I pulled her close to me again. "Hamilton, people are looking at us."

"We live in a cynical world," I said. "Let them look. It's not every day they get to see what true love really looks like."

Raiya laughed, and finally sidestepped me enough she was able to slip free. "No offense to your kisses," she said, "but I still prefer romance to be less of a public spectacle."

"I suppose Mikey's blog ruined it for you?"

"You could say that," Raiya agreed. There was a playful twinkle in her eye. "Maybe I'll remind him of that while we go see him."

"Maybe *I'll* remind him of that when we see him." I chuckled. "Why did my dad tell you he was here?"

"I heard him say to another nurse that Mikey was coming in this morning to pick up one of his school books he'd left behind."

She grinned. "He's not like you that much. He forgot he was on speaker phone with me when he said it."

"I've been saying the same thing for years," I assured her.

The time I spent with Raiya always seemed to make the rest of my life shimmer over with a haze of sorts, unless I was paying close attention.

I didn't pay attention a whole lot, I guess.

It seemed that I only had to blink, and we were already at the floor where Mikey had been staying as an outpatient for the past six months.

Raiya managed to get us through the barrage of nurses and assistants to his room, and I managed to put up a blockade on the door when I saw Mikey stuffing a book into his backpack on the bed.

"Mikey."

He glanced up at me, his brown eyes troubled. "Dinger."

"I'm guessing you weren't expecting me?" I asked.

"No," he said bitterly. "I wasn't. But then, you stopped visiting me months ago, so you really only have yourself to blame."

"I suppose that's why you thought it would be okay to tell your dad about me?"

"Grandpa told me that you weren't helping Gwen and the other victims, even though Dad and his company had found a way to cure them," Mikey insisted. "If I 'betrayed' you, it's only because you deserved it."

He turned toward Raiya. "You're no better either, if you didn't want to help," he said. "But I didn't give you up."

That was one question that was answered, at least, and it was a comforting answer.

"Grandpa Odd wasn't who he said he was," Raiya told Mikey, stepping forward. "I'm here to tell you that. I should've known, and when I did, I should've said something."

"He was always nice to me," Mikey said. "He was always looking out for me."

"He's always looked out for himself, like everyone else on the planet," I huffed.

"Like you are right now, I'm guessing?"

Ouch.

"I'm not lying," I said. "He's not a real person. He's a dragon, a changeling dragon like Elysian, who can change into human forms. He's been playing this town for decades, or possibly even longer."

"His real name is Draco," Raiya added. "And he has the power of immortality."

"Well, that's great," Mikey said. "Next you'll be telling me that Rachel's actually a sun goddess and Letty is the daughter that sprang out of her head or something."

"We're not lying."

"It doesn't matter, does it?" Mikey shot back. "Dad got what he wanted."

"Did you?" Raiya asked quietly.

He frowned at her, obviously displaced. "No," he finally said. "They captured him, and they captured me, and they set me free. It's over."

"Why did they want Hamilton?"

"I don't know," he scoffed. "Why don't you ask them?"

"Probably just for Cheryl," I told Raiya, thinking of what Dante had told me before while we were in the room together. "But Draco didn't see Cheryl stepping down from the case, or from her position as the D. A."

Frankly, I wouldn't have seen it, either.

"Martha said before they might want cooperation," I said. I looked at Mikey. Was it possible they would use him against me again, especially if I needed, as Martha had warned me, to be "convinced" to cooperate?

"I don't know why you're worried about me." Mikey scowled. "You're not worried about Gwen or anyone else."

"Draco—Grandpa to you, I guess—was lying about that," Raiya told him. "There's only one way to get Gwen back to normal, and that's to get her Soulfire from Draco."

"He has it?"

"Technically." She frowned. "We told you this before."

Mikey frowned. "Why should I believe you?"

"We wouldn't lie to you," Raiya insisted. "We *didn't* lie to you before."

I stepped forward. "There's no use in trying to convince someone who's already made up their mind," I said. "Mikey, you've been my best friend for years, and maybe—"

"Maybe I've outgrown you."

"Maybe," I admitted. "But this isn't something I would lie to you about, and you know it. If you want proof there is nothing we can do to bring Gwen back, there are only two ways to get it. And I'm not doing the one."

Raiya arched a brow. "What are you thinking?"

I'll admit, it was nice to hear her asking the questions.

"Get *your dad* to meet us," I told Mikey. "He knows who I am now. Get us together, and we'll do an experiment."

"What's the other way?" Raiya asked, curious.

"I'd say we could go break into Gwen's hospice care and see if we can heal her, but I don't think her parents would be too eager to see me again," I said. "Even if I did just get the charges against me dropped."

"I'll set up the meeting with my dad," Mikey said, interrupting Raiya and me.

"Fine." I moved out of the doorway. "Until then, you can go. But you need to stay away from Grandpa Odd if you see him again."

"Fine, whatever," Mikey grumbled as he pushed past me. "Just get out of my face."

"We've always tried to protect you," Raiya told him.

"For all the good it's done," Mikey snapped.

"If you want to put yourself out of misery," Raiya countered, "there are still plenty of demons hanging around. Draco's terrified a good amount of them with his power, but there are always some who stick around to see what they can get. If you want to join Gwen, you have a chance."

I stepped in front of Raiya. "You don't need to be that hard on him," I murmured to her, before I turned to face Mikey. "Look, I promise you that we're doing all we can right now. I'm sorry about what's happened. I really am."

"I'm tired of your apologies," Mikey said.

"Okay, well, how about a call for mercy here, huh?" I held my palms out to him, face-up and empty. "Look, I know things have deteriorated between us lately. I don't want that. Not really. We've been through harder times than this. Fighting over girls, fighting over trust, this isn't like us."

Mikey said nothing.

"I've been a bad friend to you," I continued. "And to be fair, you've been a bad one to me."

Mikey's mouth gaped.

"You broke the superhero creed," I said. "You're not supposed to tell anyone my real identity. According to most movies, you will die soon for doing just that."

"But—"

"You also broke the bro code," I said. "Now, I've broken it too, but what I'm trying to get at here is that you put my life in danger, you put Raiya in danger—and since I'm in love with her, that also doesn't look good, according to most movies—and you put our mission at risk."

Mikey regained his composure. "What are you getting at, Dinger?" he asked.

"I'm saying that *I* could easily feel justified in hurting you," I said.

"Hamilton, that's not prudent," Raiya hissed at me. "And *you* thought my tactics were bad."

"No, see," I said, "I have every incentive to hit you or harm you, and I haven't. I'm angry at you—oh, yes, I'm angry at you—but I'm not going to do something stupid about it. I'm going to forgive you."

"Forgive me?" Mikey spat.

"Yes. You know I've done wrong, but you know you've done wrong, too."

"That doesn't excuse your wrongdoing."

"That doesn't excuse yours."

"You're just trying to make yourself feel better. Like you're the better person between us."

"If you forgive me, if you show me some mercy," I said, "then we'll be even."

Mikey glared at me. "I'll have to think about it," he finally said, though it was more likely he said it because he had nothing else to say, rather than he was actually going to do it.

Still, it was a start. It was a small win for me.

"Fine. Now, can you tell us anything about Grandpa Odd?" I asked. "I want to know, so I can help protect you, and help protect others."

Mikey paused for a moment, and then he sighed. "No. He just came to visit, same as always," Mikey said. "He told me about what was happening at the Time Tower, that you weren't willing to work with Dad, and that Gwen was beginning to fade from some of the reports he'd heard at Rachel's."

"Nothing else?" I asked.

"Nothing." Mikey shook his head. "I'll call you and let you know about meeting with Dad." He narrowed his eyes. "I'm not going to trust you unless you show up for the meeting."

"Until then, can we at least have the benefit of the doubt?" Raiya asked.

"No," he retorted. "We're at an impasse. That's all."

I waited until he was out of sight before I said, "That's all we need right now."

"Maybe we should send Elysian to watch him?" Raiya suggested.

"No." I shook my head. "There's no point, now. Mikey can take care of himself. Or at least he can if he wants to. We should let him. Maybe after Draco tries to claw his soul of his body, he'll be more apt to fight alongside us rather than against us."

"You're right about that."

I laughed. "Well, it must be a day for miracles, if you're going to admit I'm right."

"We agree on a lot more than you make it sound like."

"Are you disagreeing with me about agreeing with me?"

"I'll let it slide for now," she said. "I should go out and do a patrol."

"What about me?" I asked.

"You need to get to school," she reminded me.

I groaned. "Come on, you didn't need to tell me that."

"You should go," Raiya said. "What's the point of getting that 2398 on your SATs if you're not going to get the glowing school record to back it up?"

"2398?" I asked. "I haven't gotten my scores yet."

"I was taking into account the English section you were worried about," she teased.

"I wasn't worried about it, per say."

"You still need to go," she said. "Enjoy your time at school. You never know when it'll be over."

"It'll be over next June," I retorted.

"I thought that too, once," she said. "Things don't always turn out the way we want them to."

I didn't reply to that. She had a point, but it was a vague one, and that didn't do much to persuade me. But I knew she wanted me to do well, and her love made up the difference. So I relented.

"Will you be okay on the patrol?" I asked.

"I can get Elysian to help me," Raiya said. "He came in to Rachel's this morning, you know."

"What was he doing?"

"Looking for breakfast."

"I am not completely surprised," I said. "But my mother's latest chef makes a lot of raw fish and stuff like that. I figured he would have liked that, as a dragon."

"Believe me," Raiya said with a laugh, "he vastly prefers cupcakes."

"Make sure you put whatever he eats on my tab."

"I already do that. But I don't mind. It's nice to have someone else watching out for Rachel and the café when I'm not around. I'm worried Grandpa would go after them, too. He especially knows what Rachel means to me."

I put my arm around her shoulder. "We're almost there," I said. "We just have to defeat Draco, and that's it."

"There are smaller demons around," Raiya reminded me.

"There will likely always be something we could do," I said. "But my mission was originally to recapture the Sinisters. Orpheus and Draco are just extras, and stopping Alküzor from ruling the universe seems like a reasonable thing to do. After that, everything will be easy."

"It's true that there will always be evil somewhere on Earth," Raiya agreed. "Many other demons and devils are trapped inside the fire of the earth. They're waiting there until their final judgement comes."

"You can't forget humans," I said. "There are plenty that do evil things and don't have any qualms over it."

"Yes, that is true." Raiya leaned into me. "The line between order and chaos is severed with a simple choice, as good and evil run through all human hearts."

"And Stars, too," I said, giving her a quick kiss on her forehead. We were coming up on the school, and it was time to say good-bye again. "We'll have to finish this conversation later, I guess."

Raiya gave me a rueful smile. "It appears so," she said, still bantering with me.

"See you later," I said, slowly letting her pull away from me, hesitant to go back into the world surrounding the school.

I knew Martha's class was waiting and my friends all likely needed some help with their homework, and the girls were, as always, just eager to see me.

I turned back to see Raiya as she pressed into the four-point mark on the underside of her wrist and transformed into Starry Knight. She waved to me and then took off, her radiant form darting across the cloudy April skies.

Sighing, I turned back to the school. "Alright," I told myself. "Time for the real battle of the day to begin."

☼<u>9</u>☼
Foundations

Meeting with Mikey left me feeling a mixture of hopeless and angry. I felt hopeless, I decided, because he was hopeless, and I was angry with him for being hopeless.

As much as I might've wished that to be true, the truth was more along the lines of I wanted Mikey to be safe, but he didn't want me to protect him. I was angry at him for making me care, and I was angry that I couldn't just stop caring either.

His stupidity was a liability.

But as the days passed, I was able to receive some relief. Mikey came back to school, and even though he wasn't in my classes (he fell behind on a few subjects while he was tutored in the hospital), I was able to better watch over him. Better yet, I was able to do it where he couldn't accuse me of hovering around him.

That relief was a relief in itself, even if I had to dance around Drew, Poncey, and Jason, as they all asked about why Mikey and I were fighting "this time."

I played it off as one of our usual spats, either shrugging it off or distracting them while I managed to get away without actually answering any of their questions.

Fortunately, I was not the only one who was feeling an extra dose of relief. With the SATs out of the way, there were two things on everybody's mind: Prom, and summer vacation.

With a week until prom, and five weeks until the end of the school year, the school was settling into its summertime routines quite nicely. Teachers were more cheerful, students were less stressed, and everyone was generally more agreeable.

Glancing around the classroom as we finished up, a wry smile made its way onto my face. *What a difference hope makes,* I thought. Even Brittany Taylor, who'd been one of Gwen's friends, and a friend of Samantha Carter, an irritating girl who had her soul sucked out the year before, seemed more like her normal cheerful self.

Of course, that was probably just because she was getting the chance to boss people around again, I noted. She'd been elected the head of the prom-planning committee.

It was the last period of the day when Brittany buzzed her way around the room, heading toward me. "Dinger," she called, "hang on for a sec."

"What is it?" I asked. The bell rang, signaling the end of the day, and I was more than ready to leave.

"You haven't bought your prom ticket," she said, waving a checklist of people's names who I assumed also did not buy a ticket.

"Oh," I replied. "Right."

Cheryl was supposed to fill that out and get it in.

Ugh, you just can't depend on your mother, especially right after she just vowed to be a better mother in front of the whole city.

"Okay, give me one of those papers," I said, gesturing toward the stack she carried, "and I'll bring in a check tomorrow."

"Here." She gave me the permission slip (yes, that's really a thing for prom, when most people are close enough to legal adulthood). Brittany smiled sweetly and said, "Don't forget, if you're bringing a date, you'll have to pay for her ticket, too."

"What if she's paying for her own ticket?" I asked.

"She'll need her own permission slip." Brittany handed me an extra one.

"She doesn't go to this school," I said. "She shouldn't need it."

"So you actually have a date then?"

I groaned. I knew the gossip going around, and I knew of its power. Gossip was part of the information exchange at high school, and I usually managed to pay my dues; since the end of swim season, I had nothing of any virtual importance to share with my peers.

So the Gossip Karma Queen by default had come hunting for me.

I didn't like to share information about my personal life. My public life, and even its implications, were all up for grabs. It

177

didn't matter to me, so long as it mattered to them—and so long as I knew the truth.

Despite Brittany's unwelcome inquiry, I held my ground. "Yes, I have a date. She doesn't go to this school." I passed back one of the slips. "I'm bringing her." *No matter how much she'll probably hate getting scrutinized all night by you and your cronies.*

Brittany's face scrunched up. "I heard from Poncey that you don't actually have a date, and Via told me you were going to go with her."

"First of all, that's my business," I said. "Second, I wasn't aware you were paying attention to Poncey at all, since he dissed you back in elementary school."

Brittany blushed, but she glared at me as she excused herself, saying she needed to go find Guy Fitch, another social outcast, and take care of him.

Not the most genial of confrontations, I thought as she walked away. But I had another year of high school yet, to make my political prowess known and complete. So I didn't worry.

I especially didn't feel like worrying, because I was certain the battle was almost over. Draco just had to be defeated, and while his sword and his skill gave me pause, I didn't see any future in which he would *not* be defeated.

That left me free to hold off on worrying about silly things, like social cliques and school rivalries.

I did choose to concern myself about the prom, though. (Come on, this was the first year I was allowed to go, as a junior, and it was like a rite of passage.)

Because I concerned myself with it, I decided to concern Raiya with it, too, when I headed over to see her.

She was upstairs when I came, listening to some music as she worked on her supernova painting again, with its thick strokes and fuzzy clarity.

"Looks nice," I said, well aware I was not much of judge when it came to art, at least past announcing something was either "good" or "bad."

Raiya sighed. "It'll work for now," she said, as she put it up to dry.

"You have plenty of time to work on it," I said with a shrug. I pulled out the review book for AP Gov. We were creeping closer to May, and AP tests were coming up. "This review section, on the other hand, has to be done by tomorrow, or supposedly Martha's going to be upset."

"I can't imagine Mrs. Smithe getting upset with you." Raiya smirked as she began cleaning off her brushes.

I watched her for a moment, recalling *Romeo and Juliet,* the stupid play Gwen was starring in when the Sinisters started attacking Apollo City. "I was cleaning brushes," I said.

"What was that?" Raiya pushed some hair out of her face as she glanced back at me.

"I was cleaning paintbrushes the day that you came from Rosemont to work on the set for *Romeo and Juliet*," I said. "I remember your fight with that girl."

Raiya laughed. "I'd forgotten about fighting with Courtney," she said. "I was more surprised to see you that day."

"How did you know it was me?" I asked. Awkwardness took over. "I mean, how did you know I was, you know, the same person as Almeisan?"

"It took me a while to believe it," Raiya told me. She put her brushes up. "I don't have an exact answer for you, or at least one that would make sense to a scientist or a theorist like Logan, for example. But I know that there are things that we can't see, things that can outlast time. Who we are, as people, as creations, is one of them."

"But people change," I said.

"True." She reached out and took my hands. Her fingers were strong, comforting. Capable of making beautiful things. "But despite change, we still exist."

"I guess you have a point. We're still here, even if we have different names."

"Exactly," she said, "although I'm not sure 'Astraiya' is much different from 'Raiya.'"

"Your name is technically still 'Astraiya,'" I reminded her. "My parents gave me a completely different name."

"I think with being here, it's more like a title change of sorts," Raiya said. "I mean, you can agree with me. That happens here already. You're the one who calls your mother by her first name."

"Cheryl suits her better." I thought about my mom's decision to go back to private practice. "Maybe she'll feel more like 'Mom' now that she's going to start her own firm."

Raiya gave me a smile, and for a long moment, for unclear reasons even to me, I wondered if she wanted kids. "So you think being here, in this realm, is like motherhood?" I asked.

"The logic has parallels."

"Do you think you'd like to be a mother someday?"

Her sudden stillness answered the question, and she turned away to grab a towel to clean up. I narrowed my gaze at her, calling on my power, and I was surprised to see she was afraid.

"Are you afraid of having kids?" I asked.

"No," she snapped. "I just … I just don't think of it very often."

I could sense her hesitancy, so I moved over to her and took a hold of her hands. I saw they were shaking slightly, like they had been the day she came to rescue me from Cheryl and Dante.

I knew at once what was wrong; she wasn't afraid of having kids; she was afraid of not having them, and losing them. Just like she was afraid of losing me again.

"Show me," I said.

Raiya looked at me quizzically, before I clarified. "I mean, show me how you feel about it," I said.

"Why?"

"Why not?" I countered. "Come on. I want to see what's in your heart."

Raiya tensed under my touch, but I met her gaze with my own, and I silently promised her that I could handle it.

Slowly, I felt her submission. Warmth trickled into my skin. I felt a tentative pulse, the forerunner to a strong flood underneath the initial hesitancy.

I felt the love she had for me, pressing past the limits of my knowledge and imagination. It burst through me, penetrating me, pushing into the core of my heart and being. It took strength to keep standing as I held her there. I heard the sharp release of my breath, and I felt my knees buckle slightly.

I closed my eyes; immediately, I saw the rush of images accompanying her power. I saw our past, our present, and our future, as they came together, splashing together in a world of wet darkness, wrapping around itself into a bundle of light and joy.

A heartbeat later, I saw the bundle as Raiya held it, as I held both of them, and felt a rush of pride and love so much I had to let go of her for fear I would be swamped by the vision— for fear I would willingly run into it and drown myself.

Raiya pulled back, letting my hands drop from hers. "I'd love to be a mother," she said quietly, allowing me time to reorient myself.

Even as I put my mind back into its usual order, I knew what she was really saying; she wanted to be a mother—as long as I was there with her.

"But I know that it's not something I want right now," she added, still moving away from me.

"Right," I said, finally finding my voice again.

"I don't think about it too often," she confessed. "I'm still getting used to thinking of the future, past this mission."

I nodded.

"Actually, if you're up for it, I thought about heading over to see Logan again," she said, grabbing a jacket from her desk chair. "We promised—what is it?"

As she passed me, I felt my hand reach out and take her arm. It was an awkward motion from my position, but I felt compelled.

"What is it?" Raiya asked.

I stared at my hand, suddenly wondering what exactly I should say.

I knew what I *wanted* to say. I wanted to tell her I loved that she wanted to be a mother, that she wanted to be with me. That I loved her, and I wanted that, too. That I wanted to marry her and make her my permanent home, officially, here, in this realm and in this life.

Instead of any of that, I said, "I never really wanted kids."

Before I could explain I was changing my mind about that, and about so much, really, since she'd come into my life, Elysian came into the room, walking on his hind legs.

Talk about a mood killer.

I sighed and let it go. I had a number of things to discuss with her, so I would have the chance to bring it up again.

"There you are," he said. "I was wondering where you guys were."

I dropped Raiya's arm. "What is it?" I asked.

"Dante." Elysian scowled. "He's walking toward the observatory."

"I'm just saying we should go there anyway," Raiya remarked. "Sounds like it would be a good time to check in on Logan."

"We can confront Dante in the meantime," I said. I thought about texting Mikey, but decided against it a second later. He wanted to be on his own, so I would let him. Even if he was unfit for the job in question.

Elysian, Raiya, and I all transformed in the shadows of the alley next to Rachel's, and then we took off.

We had almost arrived at Lakeview Observatory when I realized I'd forgotten to remind Raiya that the prom was this weekend. I'd gotten distracted by our talk of the future, and the vision I had of Raiya's heart.

I'll get it later, I promised myself, *along with the other stuff.*

☼10☼
Findings

Considering how I'd left Dante before, I wasn't really that excited to see him again. Of course, I don't think I was ever really happy to see him, but this time I was *especially* not that excited.

I was glad to see, however, that the Otherworld, Inc. guards seemed to have vanished, and we had no trouble slipping through the back door of the observatory.

Lakeview was still open to the public, so we had to be cautious as we walked around. More than once we all scurried around a corner or ducked into a nearby room. We walked through the bottom floors, and it was only when we came to the telescope room that we stopped.

"I don't see Logan anywhere," Raiya said.

I glanced at one of the clocks. "Maybe he's teaching down at the college tonight?" I wondered aloud. "Or grading papers or something there for one of his other professors?"

"That's true," she said with a sigh. I knew she was not completely convinced.

Dante stepped out of the shadows. "He stepped out for an early dinner with one of his colleagues from the college. You'll have to excuse him for the moment."

In one motion, we swiveled around.

"You've really got to stop doing that," I told him.

"It's practical," he said, in a smug, apologetic sort of way.

"It's irritating."

"Most irritating things are practical."

"Not necessarily." I folded my arms across my chest. "We could argue the specific points on that for a while, but let's just get down to business, shall we?"

"Fair enough."

"What are you doing here? Mikey didn't call you already, did he?"

"No," Dante replied. "I can't imagine why he would, either. I told him to stay away after we caught you."

"He doesn't listen," I said. "It's not surprising that he didn't call you, after he said he would. Did you really tell him I wasn't helping you help the people who had their Soulfire stolen—the people who have that sickness?"

"No," Dante said, "I didn't say that."

"Draco did," Raiya reminded me. "Dante just let Mikey go on the assumption, I'll bet."

"Life is complicated, and if you're lucky enough to live long enough, you'll get an idea of just how complicated it is," Dante said neutrally.

So Raiya was right.

"What are you going to do when he calls you and tells you that I'll go with you to help the victims?" I asked.

"I'll tell him what I told him before: Stay away from me," Dante said.

"He won't trust me again until we do."

"That's his problem, then, more than yours."

"It might not be enough to stop him from doing something stupid."

"You'll see to it, and I'll see to it," Dante said, "that he doesn't get caught up in this. That's why I wanted to speak with you."

"You mean," Raiya said, "that you, not SWORD, want to talk to us."

"Yes." He stepped forward and looked at me. "You know as well as I do, Hamilton, that we both have liabilities."

I agreed with him, even if I hated to hear him say that Mikey was a liability. "We can't trust you."

"I have a solution for that," Raiya said, as power glowed in her hand. She reached out to Dante. "This is my power, as the Star of Justice. Your word will bind you; if you lie to us, you will not escape your due."

"Charming," Dante muttered, but he shook her hand.

"Fine," I said. "Now, let's talk."

"I want you to leave Mikey out of this."

"Why?" I asked.

"Because he is my son," Dante said.

"You didn't seem to care about that before you left him," I pointed out.

"Do you think this is easy for me?" Dante's voice was hushed. "I have given my word not to lie to you, but I said nothing about hurting you."

"I'll say something about that," Raiya warned. Her bow was out in a flash of light.

Elysian snorted behind us. "There's no need to threaten us. It wouldn't make much of a difference, anyway," he told Dante. "The kid here is a bit slow when it comes to learning through pain."

I almost whacked him over the head for the remark, but since it technically discouraged an attack against me, I let it go. For the moment.

Dante wisely retreated. "Fine," he grumbled. "But I still need you to leave my son out of this as much as you can, and protect him if I can't."

"Fine," I repeated. We could agree on that.

"Even if it's me he needs protecting from," Dante continued, "you must stop me."

That took me aback a bit.

I guess he really is here without SWORD's approval.

189

"We agree," Raiya spoke up. Her determination, with no hesitation, startled me.

"Good," Dante said, before I could object or question him further. "Now that Mikey is off the table, I will release your identity as well."

"The rest of SWORD doesn't know who I am?" I asked.

"I have the file," he said, "and the only copy." He pulled it out of his pocket and tossed it to me. "So, no, no one else knows."

"Why are you doing this?" I asked.

"Mark is also one of my oldest friends," Dante said. "We were friends in high school. I have tried to keep him out of the loop as much as possible, but there are some things he knows, and he's in danger just from that. I think we can agree that Mark, and by extension your mother, need not be an issue between us."

"We can agree on it," I said. Glancing over at Raiya, I added, "I want Starry Knight protected, too."

"Done," Dante agreed.

Raiya looked like she was going to say something, but I shook my head. We could discuss it later.

"Now that we've come to terms," Dante said, "I'd like to hear what you know."

"About Draco, or about anything else in particular?" I asked.

"SWORD is a company that monitors power first," Dante said. "We have good resources, but there's nothing like hearing it from the other side."

So we are still on opposing sides. Right?

"It was my brother," Elysian said. "I'd tried to warn you before. Draco has been masquerading as a human for some time here in the city. He used Orpheus to weaken Time's power and to break his dragon skin free from its prison."

"He's a changeling dragon, like you?"

"One of the few," Elysian agreed. "He has an immortal life. With his power, and the power he's used from the Sinisters and the meteorite that was kept here, he's grown considerably more powerful."

"What does he want?"

"To release Alküzor and set the realm free from the Prince of Stars' power," I said. "Alküzor is trapped inside the world, but he has a lot of power, too. He wants to take over."

"I see you've started paying attention to the facts," Elysian murmured beside me.

"I always did," I said. I shot him a smirk. "I just pretended not to care to annoy you."

"Fire has a purifying effect," Dante mused. "I can see why he's been put in there, even if it would take forever to purify him."

"Draco hasn't made a move to release him," I said. "I get the feeling from when he talks to me he's holding off on it for some reason."

"Evil is better at waiting, better at hiding," Raiya said. "Goodness doesn't need to change or adapt."

"I've heard that," I said. "But it doesn't explain why he's waiting, not entirely."

"It's possible he doesn't actually want to do it," Dante said. "He's a powerful foe, and he's enjoying it. I doubt competition is something he wants."

"That might be true." I thought about what Draco had said to me before, and how he still seemed emotionally connected to Raiya. Maybe Dante had a point, but I was more inclined to think that Draco's heart wasn't completely in it.

Alora told me once that only in Time was everlasting change possible. The temporal was discarded, and the eternal was solidified. While Draco was an immortal being, was it possible that Time's power had affected him more than he realized?

"That's all we really know about Draco's intentions," Raiya said. "But we do know that he was once known as Ogden Skarmastad."

"The founder of the Skarmastad Foundation." Dante frowned.

"The guys who paid for you to be hired through Otherworld," I added.

He nodded. "But why would he play both sides?" Dante asked. "We're here to essentially stop him. SWORD's main job, right now, is to protect you." He nodded toward me, and I fought the urge to shrink back.

"Draco's always been crafty," Elysian said. He flicked his tail against the ground.

"For now," Dante said, "Otherworld, Inc. has been dropped by the city. With your mother folding on the case, and shuffling over to the private sector, we have no obligation to Apollo City anymore."

"But SWORD is still on assignment to protect and assist Wingdinger," Raiya said.

"Yes." Dante turned to me again. "You are the Star of Mercy, and you are the only one who had the power to overcome a being like Alküzor, should he get free."

"The Blood Flame," I whispered.

Dante nodded.

"So it will come down to me," I said, "if we want to save the city."

"Alküzor will still have to get through me," Raiya said.

"And Draco will not pass me," Elysian added.

I felt warmth as they surrounded me; not only were they my allies, but they were my friends. "Hopefully," I said, "it will be enough."

"It will," Dante said.

"How do you know?" I asked, wondering if he was friends with Alora, or if Adonaias had reached out to him, too.

"Fate is a funny thing, sometimes. The Skarmastad Foundation paid for SWORD to come in, not me. But I never wanted to come back here, knowing as I did the memories that awaited me once I got here. But my bosses knew I was from this area, so they arranged for me to take the lead.

"SWORD might be after power, and I can respect that, even now. But they are helpless when it comes to love. I thought power was all I needed. Turns out, power is at its most potent when it is laid down for love."

"That sounds too cliché for you to say," I said, unable to stop myself from sneering.

"Yes, well, as I said before, life is complicated," Dante grunted. "The inner lives of people are even more complex."

"Can you tell us the exact reason SWORD was hired?" Raiya asked. "You've said before they know of the Stars and other elements outside this world. Are they allied with Draco or Alküzor at all?"

"No. SWORD was hired because this is what we do— investigate and intersect the supernatural, the paranormal, etc. This is what the company has done for the past twenty years now." Dante shrugged. "We have been given a few more assignments here, and then I will depart with them."

THE STARLIGHT CHRONICLES

"Assignments like what?"

"For now," he replied, "our next assignment is to help you stop Alküzor from tearing the gates of hell open and sending the universe as we know it into a black hole of some kind. You know as well as I do—perhaps even better—that the situation has escalated and a more dangerous threat has arisen. If this is a power we can't control, we need to stop it. Or exploit it."

"Whatever serves you better," Raiya grumbled.

I could understand why she was so adamant about keeping them in the "bad guy" box, but I frowned at her. There was no need to close the door completely on SWORD or Dante, especially right now. We didn't have to be friends with someone to appreciate their help, and for the moment, our goals were aligned.

"Good to know," I said. "What about Mikey? Can you talk to him and explain that there's nothing we can do about Gwen, and the others, for now?"

"Blaming Draco for his deception will likely be enough to take care of that problem," Dante said. He hardened his gaze. "Warning him away will have to be enough to prevent any other problems."

"If he's anything like the kid here," Elysian muttered, "don't count on it."

"Elysian, I swear, you need to—"

Our conversation quickly devolved into an argument. It was only when Raiya finally managed to stop us, several moments later, that we realized Dante had slipped away.

"Great." I nearly stomped my foot in frustration. "He's gone."

"He might have had to leave," Raiya said.

"You're defending him now?"

"No," Raiya insisted, even though I could see her cheeks fluster over in the dim lighting. She cleared her throat. "I heard some movement down the hallway. Maybe he had to leave so he wouldn't be seen by other SWORD agents or by any witnesses. He did tell us that he was here without their approval or direction."

"We don't know if he was here without their knowledge," Elysian said.

The door opened before I could say anything else. Logan came in, one hand holding an open book, and the other carrying a take-out bag. He glanced up at us in surprise. "Hey guys," he said.

"Hi, Logan," Raiya said. "How are you?"

"Good," he said as he gave us a smile. "You guys must've known I was thinking of you earlier."

"I'm surprised you were thinking about us at all. We heard you were out on a date," I said.

Logan grinned. "I'm not going to confirm or deny anything about that," he said. "But before I left, a couple of things happened I thought you should know about."

"What is it?" Elysian asked.

"First, the Otherworld guys are gone," Logan said. "I got a memo about it this morning. Apparently they have been assured that the insurance company has paid out for the loss of the meteorite. So they're not worried about it getting stolen anymore."

"Considering it was stolen," I said.

"Yep," Logan replied. "No need to guard something that's not around to guard."

"Saves them some money."

"The government has never really seemed to worry about that," Elysian muttered.

He's been watching too many news channels, I thought.

"What's the second thing you wanted to tell us?" Raiya asked.

"The vortex has disappeared from my radiation maps," Logan said.

Raiya, Elysian, and I all exchanged knowing glances. That was because Draco had used the vortex for its purpose—to forge the meteorite into a sword of his own.

"But I have picked up on some traces of the radiation signature," he added.

"Can you bring it up on the screen?" Raiya asked, stepping forward. She took his bag and his book as he obliged her.

Logan keyed in a few words and seconds later, he pulled up the picture of the city maps. There were dots and shapes and colors all swirling around, like a weather map mixed in with tie-dye.

"Here," he said, gesturing toward several lines slivering their way around the northern part of the city. "The blue lines here are similar radiation patterns to those of the meteorite," he said. "It's a bit different from before, and it's more faded. I didn't see it the first couple of times I looked at it."

I squinted my eyes, looking toward the lines. "It's running through Rosemont's old site," I said.

"And the hospital, and the Time Tower, and the marina," Elysian added.

"And Rachel's," Raiya whispered.

As I silently vowed to protect my coffee kingdom, I glanced over at Logan. "What do you think it means?"

"I don't know," he admitted. "I know that the meteorite has disappeared, and by all indications it's either been destroyed or it's out of the city limits. Or out of the reach of our tracking satellites."

"Thank you for showing us," Raiya said. Her tone was gracious and her eyes were kind, but I could tell she was worried.

"I don't know if it will help you," Logan said. "But now that my research has been tanked, it's back to observation for now."

"It might help us," I said, "but I'm not entirely sure how at the moment."

"It might help if you had a degree in astrophysics and aeronautics," Elysian said.

Stop being unhelpful! I wanted to scream at him. He'd already cost me quite a bit that night—stolen moments of sweetness with Raiya and a tolerable span of time to discuss things with Dante. I didn't need him bruising my ego or stoking my temper.

Logan didn't seem to notice my irritation, but kept walking us through charts and facts and figures. Soon, I began to feel like I was in one of Mr. Hale's science courses, my body stuck in one place, and my mind adrift in a sea of numbers and symbols.

"Thanks for all your help, Logan," I heard Raiya say. "I think that's all we can handle for tonight, but it's given us a good place to start."

"I'm glad to hear it," Logan said. "I know you can't tell me everything that's going on, but I know that you're the good guys. I'm happy to help."

"We're more than grateful," I assured him.

I was telling the truth. As Logan sat down with his book and his doggie bag once more, and Elysian, Raiya, and I all headed out of the building, I couldn't help but feel like Draco's days were numbered.

"That was interesting," Raiya said. "And disturbing."

"It was all good information." I reached over and knocked Elysian on the head. "We probably could've gotten more information out of Dante if you hadn't started arguing with me."

"I didn't start the argument," Elysian grumbled. "I said something and then you started arguing with me. I'd say it's more your fault than mine."

"As usual!" I shook my head. "That's what you *always* do."

"I'm not the only one who's doing just what he always does," Elysian shot back. "You're no different!"

"How?" I asked.

"You're back to planning out your life and just dragging people along," Elysian said to me in an accusing tone.

"I have to drag you along sometimes!" I threw up my hands. "Do you know how awful it is, trying to get Starry Knight to actually live?"

"Excuse me?" Raiya interrupted. "I'm doing just fine on my own!"

"No you're not," I said. "I practically had to twist your arm about prom."

"So I don't want to 'live' unless I want to go to prom?"

"Yeah," Elysian joined in. "Where you can parade her in front of your friends as proof that your life is better than theirs?"

"What are you talking about?" I hissed at him. I turned back to Raiya. "Come on, prom is practically right up there with getting your driver's license. It's part of growing up."

"That's the difference between us," Raiya retorted. "I already have grown up—and I didn't need to go to prom to do it!"

She turned away from me and took off before I could stop her.

I whirled around, glaring at Elysian. "You didn't have to make me fight with her."

"I didn't make you do anything," he said. "*You* did all the talking."

I clenched my fists angrily. "You're just terrible!"

"So what?" Elysian asked. "You still have a problem."

"I'll say! I'm looking at it."

"You know, even if we are terrible, flawed beings," Elysian said, "that doesn't mean that we are incapable of getting things right. It doesn't mean we will do the right thing. It means we know what's right and want you to be better."

"That's stupid," I said. "Clean up your own act first."

"I will!" Elysian assured me. "And you will not like it when I do."

"You must've been hanging out with Aleia more than I thought if you're going to hurl cryptic remarks," I yelled at him.

Seconds later, he huffed loudly, sending a stream of smoke out of his nostrils, and then he flew away.

☼11☼
Prom

I went home after fighting with Elysian and Raiya. It was easier to fight against them and feel like I was the winner; fighting against myself meant that I always lost, even when I won.

It was becoming more of an issue the longer I knew both of them.

Of course, I still loved myself more. I'd known myself longer.

Or had I? I mean, less than two years ago, I didn't know I had any supernatural powers (other than getting good grades and making it look easy at the same time.)

Maybe that was what drove me from my dreaming, leaving me largely sleepless, making me even more restless and on edge than usual.

It was a good thing I was talented; the last days of the week were tense. Raiya didn't talk to me much at all, and Elysian only seemed to sniffle at me.

I was giving them room, and I assumed they were giving me room, too—room to fume, more than anything else. Room to worry, the rest of it.

One of the things I decided not to worry about was SWORD. I would get to that later, if I worried about it at all. Even if Raiya had her reservations, I thought they were basically allies now, and that was all that mattered. We still had some philosophical differences as far as I could see, but there was nothing preventing me from dealing with them after we took care of Draco. If I had to take care of them at all. Dante had said they had a few more assignments, and then they would be stepping out.

No, I was more worried about other things.

Friday was a half-day at school, as it was prom night. The school was decorated and the students were all cheerful, myself included. Poncey was practically prancing around, while Jason was cheering about finally finding a date. I was happy to hear my friends were coming—even Simon was coming, though he was bringing someone I didn't know as his date.

Mikey was the only one of us who was rather reserved. But he had other problems to worry about. Since he'd fallen behind in his schoolwork, he wasn't able to go to the prom.

But I wasn't worried about him, either. Not really, anyway. I was more worried that Raiya was going to back out of our agreement.

I hadn't been that nice to her, I supposed. She was already not excited about going to prom; I didn't need my emotion-reading skills to know that. The fact I'd hurt her didn't seem to help.

So after school, and the obligatory shout-outs to my friends and discussions with others who wanted nothing more than to be my friends, I headed over to see her.

"Hamilton." Rachel greeted me with her usual warmth. "How are you today?"

There was no hint to suggest anything was wrong.

I cheered instantly. "Hi, Rachel." I walked over to the counter where she was cleaning. "Raiya getting ready for the prom?"

"Prom?" Rachel frowned. "That's tonight?"

"Yes. Didn't I tell you about it?"

She laughed at my frightened confusion. "Just teasing," she said. "But no, Raiya had her GED this morning. She'll be finished with it in another hour."

Shame sank into me. I'd forgotten about her test!

"I forgot," I said, half in disbelief and half in annoyance.

At least nothing happened while she was taking her test, I thought.

"I think she did, too," Rachel admitted. "I came in early this morning so she could go. She was running behind schedule. She seemed distracted." Rachel gave me a teasing glance. "She seems to be distracted a lot when you come around now."

I grinned, despite feeling bad about forgetting her.

"You really do love her, don't you?" Rachel asked.

"Of course," I said. "Even if I forget about her tests."

"Good." Rachel handed me my cup. "There's nothing like love to add magic to a special night like this. Go home and get ready for tonight. By the time you're ready, she'll be ready, too."

I agreed. I left, feeling better knowing Raiya wasn't going to leave me hanging. Rachel would see to that.

For all of Rachel's more annoying fluffy true love stuff, I was glad she was like that—and not just because it meant I could count on her to help me in certain instances like this one.

As I changed my clothes and showered, I got a voicemail from Cheryl, who, even though she wasn't working, was held up at a meeting with a potential investor for her firm.

I suppose many parents take pictures and gush over their kids at prom, but I didn't have to deal with that. Adam was the only one who seemed excited for me; he took pretend pictures of me as I came down into the living room with his toy camera, while Mark dozed in the armchair. Even Elysian seemed to be missing, but considering his fondness for sweets and his concern over Draco, I had a few ideas of where he was.

"Boy."

I turned to see Ayako poking her head out from the kitchen. She had a real camera in her hand. "Let me take picture for you."

"Alright."

THE STARLIGHT CHRONICLES

A few pictures later, she slipped me a nice surprise: A corsage. "For your lady," she said with a kind smile.

I regretted, for a teeny tiny moment, that I'd been so harsh on Ayako's cooking. Just because she didn't make food I liked didn't mean she wasn't a nice person. Maybe that was true of the others, too, and I'd just been unable, or unwilling, to see it.

The corsage in itself was pretty; there was a large white bloom, surrounded by small pink blossoms, with a nice arrangement of baby's breath and small decorative inserts.

I didn't know the names of the flowers, nor did I care much.

"Thank you," I told the kind cook, giving her a quick kiss on the cheek.

"Oh, sweet boy," she said with a small chuckle. "Go have fun."

I didn't need any more prompting. I hurried outside, surprised to find Elysian, clearly waiting for me. I didn't know if it was the weather or his presence, but all of a sudden there seemed to be a chill in the air.

"What are you doing here?" I asked.

"Starry Knight asked me to come and get you," he said.

"I didn't feel anything," I said, glancing down the mark on my wrist. "Is something wrong?"

"No," he said. "She's getting ready for prom, and I was bothering her, so she sent me on this errand to get rid of me."

I laughed. "She's smart."

"She also figured this would give you a chance to apologize to me," Elysian said.

I stopped laughing. "She's diabolical," I muttered.

"So I guess that's a no-go on the apology?"

"What do I have to apologize for?"

"For your general selfishness, maybe?" Elysian shrugged. "At this point, the list is so long I don't think I could read through it all."

"If you're supposed to take me over to Raiya's," I said, my tone low and dangerous, "you'd better stop talking."

"You don't make it easy," he snapped. "Your life is always just one long to-do list, and you act like we're pitted against you when we don't think a certain way or fall into line behind your expectations."

"My expectations are *reasonable*," I argued, starting to walk down the road, out of the subdivision and toward the coffeehouse café.

"Your arrogance is not," Elysian muttered behind me.

"What about your arrogance?" I said. "You're the one who's judging me."

"I've seen the kind of behavior you have before," Elysian reminded me. "Draco was just like you, even before he chose to rebel along with Alküzor and the others."

"I'm not like him."

"Yes, you are." Elysian pushed back. "You're all about yourself, and you don't mind running the people who care about you over if it means you get your way."

He scurried ahead of me, and we dropped the subject along with the conversation.

I rebelled against his reasoning, but I had to wonder at him. *Did Elysian just admit he cared about me?*

Despite my anger over Elysian's accusations, I made a promise to myself to be nicer to him. I didn't want to apologize—seriously, the end of the world would happen before I willingly apologized to him first—but I could forgive him for being a jerk about things.

After all, I thought, Draco's betrayal had to have hit him hard. While Elysian and I weren't brothers, we were brothers in arms, and we had a mission to face together. He could have easily been hesitant to trust me because of the past.

It didn't excuse his behavior, but it explained it better.

I forgot about Draco and Elysian as we arrived at Rachel's. The corsage was in my hand, and I was surprised to feel a bit nervous.

Rachel waved to me from the back as we walked in. "Hey!" she called. "Raiya's upstairs."

"Thanks," I called back.

I turned to Elysian. "Stay down here, out of sight," I said. "I'm going to go get Raiya."

"Fine. Hurry up. I'm hungry," he muttered.

"Don't you mean, 'take your time,' then?" I asked. "Raiya already told me she puts whatever you eat on my tab."

Elysian thought this over for a moment. "Good point," he finally said, and then he slithered out of sight, already changing into a chameleon-like form as he headed toward the kitchen.

I let him go and allowed my nerves to resume their persistent hum. My nerves doubled the instant I walked up to Raiya's room and saw her.

She was wearing the dress she'd worn for Rachel's wedding. I recognized it instantly, and not just because of what it looked like; I felt the same rush of reaction, the same admiration I felt for her last summer. Of course, this time it was much more potent, because I let myself admit I was attracted to her.

Her hair was pulled back in a half-bun, no doubt a nod to her Starry Knight persona. There was even a line of small flowers in her hair where the wings on her head normally sat.

As I caught her eye, she winked at me.

I stood up straighter and made sure my mouth hadn't dropped open in shock.

She came up to me and slid her arm through mine. "Rachel wants to get some pictures," she warned me.

I pretended to groan. "We have a long night ahead of us, then."

"You could end it right now," Raiya offered. "It would spare me a lot of embarrassment in front of your friends."

"You're the one who told me everything was going to be alright," I reminded her. I showed her the corsage Ayako had given to me. "You're going to have to prove to me you know it this time."

I pinned it to her dress, careful not to poke her, and stepped back. "There," I said, leaning forward to give her a kiss on the cheek. "You're mine."

As she blushed, I felt the desire behind her eyes as she looked back at me. No amount of Starlight defender training in the world could've prepared me to resist her silent plea.

The instant I allowed myself to lean in and kiss her, I felt the rest of my resistance disappear. My hands were suddenly tangled in her hair, my mouth fused to hers, and her body pressed against mine.

She welcomed me, her hands running down my back as she tried to pull me closer. We stumbled against each other, and I barely managed to catch us against the wall. I was too intoxicated at the taste of her, the feel of her, the heat between us—all of it overwhelmed me, and I was unable to do anything more. Everything washed over me, leaving nothing behind. Nothing but her.

"Hamilton," she whispered as she began to push me away. "We're going to be late."

"It's okay," I insisted.

"But—"

"Please," I begged. "Please, just let me kiss you for a bit longer."

We'd had this discussion before, several times. I knew she was hesitant when it came to passion, and I knew she had good reason to be—she hadn't been thinking clearly when Orpheus tricked her into going supernova on the other side of Time, and the possibility of losing me again terrified her.

So when she relaxed and gave me a tremulous smile, I felt the weight of her trust and the burden of her hope as they broke through my yearning.

"Okay," she whispered, leaning forward to kiss me again. "But Rachel still wants pictures. We can't be too much longer, or she'll come looking for us."

I barely heard her as I kissed her throat. "Okay," I said, savoring her shock at the tender caress.

I wasn't sure how much time passed before we were interrupted; I only knew that it was too short of a time. I nearly fell over in surprise when Rachel knocked on the door.

"I did warn you," Raiya said with a giggle. Her arms pulled back from me, moving to straighten her hair and smooth the wrinkles out of her dress.

I was only a little disappointed to see the corsage I'd given her was crushed.

"Fair enough," I replied, trying to catch my breath as well as my balance.

Rachel came in just as I managed to steady myself.

"There you are," she said. "It's almost time for the prom to start."

"We're ready," I said, grabbing Raiya's hand.

"Great! Let me get some pictures and then you guys can head out." Rachel grinned. "Do you want a coat, Raiya? I heard on the news it's supposed to snow tonight."

"Snow?" I asked.

"It's an onion snow," Rachel explained. "They come sometimes, at the end of April or the beginning of May. The temperature's been dipping since earlier, so I thought I'd warn you."

Huh, I guess it was the weather earlier, rather than Elysian. I was surprised.

"I'm okay," Raiya said. "I don't think I'll need a coat."

"She can have mine," I said, tugging at my suit, "if she needs it."

Once I stepped outside, I realized Rachel was right. *The downside of being a Star,* I thought. *I could no longer appropriately dress for the weather on my own.*

I was comforted that I had all the warmth I would need. Raiya was beside me, and a night of adventure was ahead of us.

"Ready to go?" I asked her.

She gave me a quick smirk. "It would be my pleasure," she assured me.

☼12☼
Last Dance

When you are popular, especially in high school, it is necessary to have some contingency plans. You never know when your ex-girlfriend will launch herself at you, trying to convince you it was all your fault you ran into her, because you were still in love with her (to which you respond, "I was never in love with you"). You'll also likely never expect your friends to stare at your date in disbelief, making her increasingly uncomfortable, to the point where she asks you if it was time to leave just fifteen minutes after finally getting into the main room.

The prom was set up in a small conference hall close to the marina. We could see some of the ships coming in and going out as we waited in the welcoming line.

The theme was "A Night on the Sea," probably loosely based on the Titanic, guessing from some of the decorations. I didn't bother to dress up in anything nautical, and I was glad to see I wasn't the only one who hadn't bothered to learn the theme ahead of time.

But despite some of the tackier elements, there were some really nice furnishings, and the setup for the dance floor was nice. As I've said before, credit where it's due.

Raiya's hand stayed firmly in mine, but I could feel her fingertips digging into my hand every time Poncey or Drew looked at her, as if they weren't sure if I'd been telling the truth about her identity.

Jason, for his part, welcomed her, and even complimented her nicely, which set her a little more at ease. He'd seen her around Rachel's enough that he knew who she was, and I suspected he knew we'd been close for some time.

"Good job, man," he said, slapping me on the back as Brittany began chatting with Raiya about her GED.

"Thanks," I murmured back.

"I thought you might bring her," Jason added. "Rachel's been bubbly and ecstatic all week, but she wouldn't tell me who Raiya was going with to the prom."

"Well, that's Rachel for you," I remarked. "A sucker for true love if I ever saw one."

"True enough," Jason said.

"Brittany seems like an odd choice," I said.

"Hey, I complimented you."

"We're friends. I'm allowed to ask you awkward questions and say less than nice things."

Jason grimaced. "I didn't have a date, and I thought it would be a nice event. See if I couldn't smooth over her Poncey-hatred."

"Did it work?"

"I'll let you know later," he said with a grin.

I didn't want to know what he meant by that. Thankfully, I was distracted as Simon came along and met us with his date, a senior girl, but one I didn't recognize. I think she said her name was Casey or something similar.

She was nice enough, joining in with our conversations about the latest music, food, entertainment, etc. Felicia, Poncey's date, heralded us with tales of his success in their cooking elective, which was how they met, apparently.

Simon had to be on his toes some, I noticed, when his younger sister, Phoebe, arrived and met up with Drew, who was her date. He eventually calmed down some, but he made sure he was close enough to them that they never left his sight.

We talked, we ate, we took plenty of pictures, and we celebrated.

I didn't get many more questions about Raiya from the guys, so long as she was nearby. When she went to go get some punch, Drew came up to me and asked me if that was really the Raiya I'd told him all the stories about.

"I didn't hire someone to play her," I retorted. "Is it so hard to believe?"

"No," he admitted. "Just surprising."

"Why?"

"You didn't seem to like her very much. I mean, don't get me wrong, she's cute, but … "

I half-listened as Drew started reiterating some of my more pompous arguments I'd mentioned to him, recounting some of our more tense disputes from Mrs. Smithe's class and even

217

some from Mrs. Night's class. (How old was this information, exactly?)

As he continued to let them roll off his tongue, I glanced over at Raiya. She seemed to sense my gaze, and turned to give me one back. Her eyes were bright and her smile was immediate, as she saw me. I held her eyes until she finally turned away, her cheeks flushed over with crimson.

But I'd seen it—the look of pride on her face, the warmth and approval in her gaze.

Hearing my complaints against her almost made me laugh, half in amusement and half in horror. I was suddenly taken aback by my own selfishness. I'd wanted comfort in telling my friends about the arguments, but I knew I was wrong in some of them, at least, and my friends were all wrong to say nothing about my bias.

I saw now that having Raiya there was the best thing I could ever have, and I didn't want her to ever leave.

"You know what, Drew?" I said. "You're right. I don't like her. I love her."

I didn't have to turn my head to see the shock coming off of his expression. His surprise gave me a push of confidence, and I made my decision the moment I heard the music slow its tempo. "Now," I said, "I'm going to go dance with her. If you'll excuse me … "

Raiya met me halfway in the middle of the dance floor. "What are you doing?" she asked.

I plucked the drink out of her hand and passed it to some other person, who, in recognizing me, mindlessly took it. "I'd like to ask you to dance," I said.

"You're not really asking if you're not really giving me a choice." There was a bit of a smile on her face, and I knew she was arguing with me in a friendly manner.

"I can't risk you making me look like a fool," I said.

"You're not risking that at all, by asking me to dance," Raiya said.

"So you'll say yes?"

"If you ask."

"Okay. Will you dance with me?"

"No." She laughed as I cocked an eyebrow. "Just kidding." She took my extended hand in hers, and while I didn't really do any dancing, I led her around the floor in a respectable-looking pattern.

"I've never really been to a dance," Raiya admitted. "Rachel has music nights sometimes at the café, but I avoid them."

"I don't really dance at these things, much," I told her. "So you're in good company."

"The best," Raiya said with a grin. I was more gratified when she took a step closer to me. Her eyes met mine, as her lips were only inches away.

"Are you nervous?" I asked.

"Why would I be nervous?" she asked, even as I knew she was, and she was only trying to put on a good face for me.

"Because people are staring at us," I said. I nodded toward the crowd of people around us, as several people—some friends, some frenemies, all busybodies—tried to look casual when they looked our way.

"Oh. Well, I'm better than what I thought I would be," Raiya replied. "Your friends aren't so bad, I guess."

"That's what I thought, too." I laughed.

I held her close for a few long moments. As the music died down, I sighed. I was all happy, except for one, nagging reminder, and I knew I had to do something about it.

"What is it?" she asked.

"I'm sorry," I said. "I'm sorry about fighting with you so much lately."

"Let's just say that we were both a little wrong. I know there's nothing wrong with having fun, but I got defensive when you pushed it on me. And I know this was important to you," Raiya told me. Her voice was quiet and steady, and she was talking to me like a mother would talk to her toddler after having a tantrum. I had a feeling I deserved it.

"It's not as important to me as you are," I insisted. "And it's definitely not as important as protecting the city from Draco."

THE STARLIGHT CHRONICLES

She smiled. "Thank you." Raiya leaned over and tucked her head into the crook of my collarbone, snuggling closer to me. "It's alright."

"I don't always like fighting with you."

"I know. You lose sometimes."

"I don't mean just that," I told her. "I mean, I hate it when we argue to the point where we hate each other."

"You and I have a long history of each other," she reminded me. "Practically none of it has to do with hating each other. A lot more of it has everything to do with loving each other despite our disagreements."

I suddenly wished I could remember more of all of our lives together; I barely remembered her at all, and the little I knew of my time up on the other side of Time, it had all been through Alora and Aleia's information, and some of St. Brendan's, too.

Raiya continued. "We never had to worry about this before we came to Earth," she said. "And maybe it's a good thing, to have our affection tested."

"You think it's a good thing?" I asked. "Even when I'm arguing with you?"

"In some ways. Even truth has to be tested against the evidence in court," she pointed out. "Can our affection outlast our anger and pride?"

"Yes, it can," I affirmed.

"Then it will." Raiya leaned further up and placed a gentle kiss on my cheek. "Life will test every part of us, to find what is good and what will last. I think saying you're sorry is a good way to pass that test."

"Are you going to pass it too?" I asked.

"I'm sorry," she conceded, though I thought I saw her roll her eyes, "if you thought I was angry enough to stop loving you."

"Thank you."

I clung to her as the music's last note faded away into nothing. "I'll work on trying to be better. I don't want to keep forgetting our lives are both here, and past, and ahead of us, all at the same time."

The world is a strange place sometimes. At that moment, I could see the full arc of our story; I could see Raiya by my side as I studied at Pitt, facing down a tight schedule. I could see her coming along with me when we moved, arguing down the cost of labor and the rental fee from the moving company. I could even see her, standing beside me as we were married, facing down a lifetime of arguing over the TV remote, paying off our bills, and balancing holiday plans— and still saying "I do" an infinite amount of times.

Suddenly, the decision hit me hard and fast. But it was the right thing to do, and I knew it.

I took her hand. "Come with me," I said, leading her out of the ballroom.

I headed out toward one of the small patios off to the side. I opted for one that was close to the water, under the moonlight, reflecting the stars through the thick cloud cover.

I can't believe I am going to do this, I thought. But I was turning eighteen in just a few days, and that would make me a legal adult.

It couldn't be that bad. My dad managed to get my mom to say yes, right? And less deserving people than me married all the time. Just look at Hollywood.

I had nothing to lose in asking her, and a lifetime of everything to gain.

And it wasn't like Raiya would say no.

We reached the outside, and I saw her briefly shiver at the breeze. Even I felt its sting this time, but I decided ultimately it wouldn't bother me; I was more concerned with other matters.

I smiled at her, knowing at once it was true. We were here, together, in this place, public with our love, and we both looked good in our prom clothes.

True, I didn't have a ring, but I had something I knew she would value just as much and guard just as zealously: My pride.

Hey, she's the one who said before it doesn't count unless you suffer.

Raiya glanced up at me, a quizzical look on her face. "Why did you want to come out here?"

I took her hand and tried not to shake. I took a deep breath, hoping my years of just winging important speeches would save me once more, giving me the greatest impromptu speech I would ever muster—

Only to have the shock of my life, as my wrist burned with blackened pain.

"No." I shook my head, wanting to howl in pain and raise my fist against the unfairness of the world. "No, not now."

"What is it?" Raiya asked, and then she stilled. "Draco."

"Yes," I grumbled. "He's back."

☼<u>13</u>☼
Fight of Destiny

As we turned, another vortex formed over the city, this time encasing it in a crystalline bubble. I felt Time's pull shift dramatically away from us, as though it was tearing the fabric of space-time apart.

A *boom!* echoed throughout the night, and then cut off as sharp and quickly as it had come.

I watched the rumble of the world around us stop completely, and I knew we were in big trouble.

Raiya gripped me. "Are you alright?" she asked. "Can you move?"

"Yes." I looked over at her. "Why? What's wrong?"

"He's disrupted Alora's connection to this world," Raiya explained. She pointed at the bubble-shield being conjured up in the sky before us. "He's stopped her power from affecting us. Only those of us who have been born outside of time can move now."

I glanced around to see she was right. The explosion I heard had stopped, mid-boom, right where Rosemont Academy ruins once stood. Flames, stilled yet slowing and splintering, rose out of the ground.

"We need to transform."

Her statement washed over me, and at that moment, I realized how loudly she was speaking; the explosion was deafening. My ears popped open.

Without another nudge, I pressed into the mark on my wrist, watching as the blood-red mark glowed.

Seconds later, I was no longer looking at Raiya; I was staring into the violent eyes of Starry Knight, my co-defender and trusted ally.

"Wait," I said, before she could take off.

"What is it? We don't have a lot of time," she warned me.

"I know." I sighed. "When this is over, I have something I want to ask you, alright?"

She stilled, blushed, and then she nodded. "Alright." She took my hand and tugged me along as we took off.

Elysian met us in midair. "It's Draco! He's gained enough power that he's already broken through Time's power."

"We kinda figured that it was Draco," I said.

"Where is he?" Raiya asked. Her bow flashed out, and I was pulled back into the moment before, when he fought with us as he forged his sword.

Suddenly, I knew I had to stop her. "Starry Knight," I called out, as Elysian turned his attention toward the center of the vortex.

"What?" she asked. "I thought we agreed you can talk to me about other stuff later."

"It's not that," I grunted, regretting all over again Draco's timing. I pointed to her bow. "I don't want you to worry about taking Draco out."

"What?" Both Elysian and Raiya objected.

"I mean it," I said. "Look, I'm the Star of Mercy. I know your grandfather-turned-evil-dragon-puppet is still important to you. I'm going to be the one who takes him out."

Elysian snorted. "Good luck with that."

"I'll call dibs if needed," I told her. "I could use your help distracting him. I think that would work best anyway; when we fought him before, after he revealed himself, he still seemed affected by you, too."

"You really think so?" Raiya's voice was soft against the building winds.

"I can't imagine an immortal life like his is full of friendships." Some part of me couldn't believe I was actually feeling empathetic toward Draco. I felt better knowing I was using it to destroy him, preventing him from hurting Raiya and other people ever again.

And I'm working to free the remaining Soulfire, I remembered, thinking of Gwen and Mikey.

Elysian nodded. "Alright," he said. "It makes sense. He's only connected to Starry Knight and me, so the kid—"

"Boss," I interrupted, correcting him.

"—will be the better opponent for him, if we want to win."

"Of course, we want to win," I exclaimed.

"I don't think we can *really* win this war," Elysian said darkly, his yellow-green eyes dimming as the sky was shut off from the rest of the city.

"We have to," I yelled back.

"Then get ready," Raiya said. "He's coming this way."

I scanned my field of vision. A spark on the horizon came into view, and then there was no mistaking him: Draco was flying down toward us, his sword out, his power ready.

I pulled my sword out as well. "Alright," I said. "Let's go!"

Elysian and Raiya took off, heading to meet him from different sides.

I almost took off to join them when I caught sight of the bright light blinking at me. I squinted down onto the ground, where I saw Dante was running up from the marina, hailing me.

As Raiya and Elysian met Draco in battle, I hurried down to see Dante.

He was freezing over, his body cut off from Time's power.

"Dante," I called. "What is it?"

"You," he said. "You have to stop him."

"We know that!" At his hardly-new information, I nearly hit him for calling me away from the fight.

"No," he said. "*You* have to stop him."

"I know that, too," I cried. "I was just about to go and stop him when you called me down here—"

"No," Dante said. "That's not what I mean. You have to stop him from ripping the world away out of this realm and you have to stop him from freeing Alküzor. You can do this by releasing the Blood Flame."

"Okay … " I was starting to get weirded out. "And I can do this by—"

"To release it completely, you'll have to die."

His words slammed into me. *What?!*

Dante breathed in deeply. "SWORD is not able to withstand this pressure," he said. "We are—I am—not able to help you."

"I have to die?" I repeated. I couldn't get past that part. I looked back up at Raiya, who clashed in the air once more with Draco, as he met her, his sword against her bow.

Elysian roared, letting the flames of his celestial fire heat up the sky, adding spirals of fire to crawl across the crystalline ceiling of Draco's bubble.

I turned back to Dante, watching as the last of his body froze over, falling away into the trap of a forever moment.

Helplessness suddenly came over me. *I have to die?*

"Boss!" Elysian called. "Are you coming or not?"

I turned toward him. "Coming," I called back, not sure if I would.

As helplessness fell around me, a memory suddenly called to me—the memory of the first time I met Adonaias.

I had felt a similar way; like I was going to die, but much more so that I wasn't going to live. My fear had strangled me, wrapped me up, and sentenced me to a life of slavery to the self, to the endless service of selfish fear

There had been little hope, no help.

And then, all of a sudden, there he was, calling out the power I had inside of me to prove me wrong.

I have to believe that there's still hope.

I looked at Raiya, as she faltered from one of Draco's attacks.

And then it all made sense—to me, at least. I had wished to go here, to follow Raiya to Earth, after she damned herself. Our enemies had been captured within Time for us to subdue, and now, as I faced down the greater foe, I knew I could stop him. There was a power inside of me that had been freed and tamed and strengthened through its growth and discipline. And I knew I could be saved—hadn't I already been, by Adonaias? I would be, again, by Raiya's power.

All this full circle was bound by a power driven to be overcome by love.

I saw it, and it was a thing of beauty.

My fingers tightened around the hilt of my sword, and I narrowed my wings in determination.

Raiya swept herself aside as I flew into the battle foreground. My sword came up, swinging hard and fast.

It met Draco's with a resounding *clang*, moving a gigantic force of energy between us. The clash went through me, pushing me back even as I refused to move.

Draco frowned underneath the sheer weight of my power. "Been practicing since last time, have you, lad?"

I couldn't answer him; my jaw was set, continuing to stream power at him, until he relented.

For a long second, I wasn't sure if he would give up or not. I wasn't sure if I would give up or not, either.

At last, a moment later, Elysian roared, sending another burning burst of fire our way.

I shouted in triumph, as Draco stepped back to avoid the flames. I pushed through a second after, holding him back again.

He managed to rebound, enough to where I knew I wouldn't be able to keep up the pace if this continued.

An idea hit me.

"Starry Knight!" I called. "I need to you shot an arrow at my sword!"

"Why?" she yelled back.

"Just do it!"

She looked frightened, and for a moment I didn't know if it was for me or for Draco. Even as far apart as I was from her, I knew the second she decided to do as I asked.

"I love you," I whispered to her as she drew back the arrow in her bow.

"I trust you," she whispered back. And then she released her arrow.

It sliced through the air, headed toward my sword; it moved through the air seamlessly, perfectly. Still concentrating on pushing back Draco's sword, I had to move quickly. I couldn't mess this up.

I only have one chance for this …

Draco laughed, even as it came barreling toward us. I grinned. At the last second, I stuck my arm out toward the arrow. It struck me hard, slicing open my skin and sending a trickle of blood down my arm.

I saw Draco jump back from me at once. He nearly dropped his sword in surprise, and I took advantage of his momentary weakness.

"Augh!" I lunged forward, bringing my blade down on his arm.

I grimaced as my sword struck him; he was more human than the Sinisters had been. I felt the shock of hurting another person like me, and I stumbled back.

I heard Raiya call out to me, and Elysian cheering. But I didn't pay attention to them. I was too focused on Draco.

"You'll lose this battle," I declared, bringing my sword back up to the ready as I breathed in deeply, trying harder to steady myself.

Draco stepped back, and I watched, grimly, as his arm fell to the ground and his blood, black as a demon's, came rushing out.

Despite this, there was a smile on his face. "Haven't you figured it out yet, young Hamilton?" He laughed. "Evil doesn't die; even if you destroy me, you will always find evil waiting, just waiting, to rise up in a new form."

"I'll settle for a new form," I shot back. "So long as it's not you."

I swung my sword again, this time calling forth the power of my soul. I felt it mix with my blood and burn, and I knew this was the moment—this was the moment where I could seal him away and save the day.

My sword swished through the air, only momentarily clipping him on his side as he stepped just out of reach. Immediately, I pushed forward, but he surprised me by ducking out of my way and diving toward the ground.

For the split-second I saw him, I felt a rush of relief; there was nothing underneath us but the sunken ground where Rosemont formerly stood.

It has to be over now.

Raiya's cry changed all of that.

"We have to stop him!" she said, as she hurried past me.

"Watch out, boss," Elysian called, as he tackled me just before the vortex's center came reeling toward us, following Draco and Starry Knight toward the ground.

"Starry Knight!" I cried.

"She'll be fine," Elysian snapped. "I'll get her." He hurried toward the ground as I shoved my sword into its scabbard.

From the angle I was at, I could see Draco was not going to make it; he was going to fly straight into the ground, sword first, closely followed by his head.

He isn't going to survive that, I thought. Surely not.

The image of Orpheus' sacrifice soared into my mind, and I realized Raiya was right; Draco wasn't concerned with survival anymore. Now, it was only about winning.

What better way for him to win than to die setting Alküzor free?

That makes his taunting make a bit more sense.

Coming to my senses, I followed Elysian down; despite the large dragon butt in my face, I never took my focus off of Draco.

I could see him bleeding out as he thrust his sword into the heart of the darkened ground—the sword made out of meteorite rock and demon power, forged from the fires of a celestial dragon, capable of standing up to the power of my Sealing Sword.

There was a hollow ringing noise that sounded out, as though the heart of the earth had been pierced.

"No!" I cried.

It was too late. I was too late.

☼14☼
The Void

Elysian managed to use his tail to grab a hold of Starry Knight at the last moment, before the power of the vortex began to collapse on us. He flung her into me, and he managed to catch both of us as we felt the pressure of Draco's bubble suffocating us.

The center point of the vortex came crashing down on top of the sword; Draco let go of it with his good arm only seconds before the power rushed behind him.

The earth groaned, and I could hear its cry of anger and tiredness. I could hear its guttural call for rest, for peace, for salvation—only to be met with the crack of the voided lightning, the power behind Draco's vortex, as it further divided the world into pieces.

The ground sunk even further in as the vortex pressed the sword into the ground like a wedge. From the split halves of the ground, I saw something that looked like a black hole rising up between them.

It's the void. Alküzor is coming.

Raiya, after she unwrapped herself from Elysian's tail, came over to me. I felt her fingers dig into my skin, as she grabbed onto me. "What do we do?" she asked.

It was surprising to see *she* was at a loss. I stared at her blankly, until I felt the rush of her power around my arm.

236

"No, don't do that," I told her. "I can use my blood and my Soulfire to purify the void that's breaking through. Alküzor can't come through if there's something blocking his way."

"I'm going with you," Raiya declared. "It'll be dangerous, but we'll face it together."

Before I could tell her that was the plan, if we were both going to survive, a force from behind knocked me over and out of her reach.

"Didn't forget about me, did you?" Draco grinned as he glanced toward the sword in the ground. "Soon, Alküzor will be free, and I will be at his right hand."

"We can still stop you," I told him, drawing my sword out for battle once more.

"It doesn't matter what you do now," Draco said. "My mission has been fulfilled."

I glared at him. "We'll see about that."

"We will indeed," Draco said, as he transformed. His human-like form glowed with a bright, angry black, and seconds later, I watched as his dragon form took shape.

He was still missing an arm, and he had a gash in his side to rival the one he left on Elysian before.

I saw Raiya unleash another arrow, aiming close to his eyes; Elysian fired a ball of dragon's fire at him, and I took up my sword, flying up as close to his wound as I could.

All of us began to fight, unleashing our power and helping each other out. For a few moments, as tired and sweaty as I was getting, I felt the relief of winning a battle inside of me, and one I shared with my friends. Raiya, Elysian, and I had all had moments where we were never completely in sync with each other. The fight with Draco, while the world was tearing apart and we could hear the looming roar of a demon encased in the fires of the earth, was among our finest moments as a team.

The vortex's power continued to fall into the hole forming in the earth. I wasn't expecting Alküzor to come, or I wasn't paying attention at least, because when his arm jutted out of the ground, I cried out in shock.

"Augh! What is that thing?"

A grisly ghost of an arm, covered in fire and ash, salting the air with sulfur, reached out and lashed power enough to rival gravity's revenge.

"Watch it," Raiya called. She turned her attention to the arm, shooting several arrows. I saw she followed my example, slicing open her palms and saturating them with blood, so it would be easier to seal away the demonic powers.

"Be careful," I called back. "I don't want you to—"

Before I could finish my sentence, Draco's tail wrapped around me and squeezed. "I don't want you to worry about fighting anymore," he finished for me.

Frankly, it was a great mischaracterization of words, and I almost sighed as he said it.

But that wasn't the only thing that was mischaracterized.

Elysian shot up out of the shadows and tackled Draco. Using his teeth, he managed to pull Draco's tail away from me.

Draco roared and let out a beam of his own dragon's fire. It was entrenched in lightning, with fire swirling devilishly in between the forks of twisting light. Elysian and Draco fell into a beastly battle.

"Go help Starry Knight," Elysian called, as he managed to (briefly) tie Draco down.

I watched as Draco's bloody stump smooshed into his face. "Are you sure?" I asked.

"Go!" Elysian ordered.

There was no doubt in his voice, and I heeded his call.

Hurrying over, I saw Starry Knight digging her feet into the ground where Alküzor's various body parts and power kept exploding free; she was trying hard to get closer without getting sucked down into the void.

"Raiya," I called. She reached out for me, and I grabbed her hand eagerly. In the fiercest hub of our battle, her warmth became life-sustaining for me—and she wasn't even using her healing powers.

"We've got to close up the break," she said. "Draco's sword managed to pierce into the next realm. If Alküzor escapes, he could use it to break us completely away from Time."

"What would happen then?" I asked.

"I don't want to know!" she insisted.

"So how do we stop it?" I yelled back. The gravitational pull toward the hellish opening increased, making us dig into the ground even more fiercely.

She cried out as Elysian and Draco rolled overhead, their snakelike bodies whipping around each other in a deadly dance. I grabbed her hand and felt the trickle of oozing blood.

The Blood Flame.

I knew what I had to do all of a sudden. I grabbed my sword. "Give me your hand," I said.

It was hard to maintain my balance and coat the sword with our blood, but I managed it. I tucked my sword into my one hand, and then I grabbed one of hers with my other. "Stay with me," I called.

"I will," she said. "I promise." Her fingers wound around mine, and there was a new power that flowed between us.

"Get ready to get sucked in," I said. "On three?"

"Three's good," she said.

"One ... Two ... "

"If we don't make it out of here," she said, "I'll be waiting for you on the other side. Assuming I make it there."

"Raiya," I breathed. "There's nothing Adonaias and I want more."

"I love you."

"I love you, too," I said. "But we're going to make it out of here, just like you're going to get forgiven by the Prince. All we have to do now is believe. How hard can that be?"

"Right." She grimaced, as if she knew I was pretty sure I was going to die if any part of this went wrong.

I was about to say, "three," when it happened. I felt a new, familiar rush of power.

"There's something more you can do." A voice spoke to us, calming the winds around us.

Adonaias appeared between us. "Do not let go of each other," he ordered. "When you go in, you will be tempted to let go. But I tell you the truth, you must remain together."

For a long moment, Raiya just gaped at him. "Adonaias," she finally said, gasping out his name.

"Astraiya." He greeted her warmly, reminding me of a father who was welcoming his daughter home. "Follow his lead and stay with him."

She clung to my hand, but she also reached out for his. Her hand went right through him, as if he was a hologram or a projection. She stepped back.

"I am with you in spirit," he explained patiently.

Raiya nodded and steadied herself. "Does this mean I'll get a new wish?" she asked him.

I almost yelled at her for asking for such a trivial thing when we had Alküzor to stop and the world to repair, but I couldn't. One look at the desperate, disbelieving love on her face, and I knew I would have thrown the world away for her if it meant she was welcomed into the Celestial Kingdom again.

"No," Adonaias told her. "I have something better for you. But you will not receive it until you are willing to let go of your own wish."

"But, what—"

"Are you going to just stand there?" Elysian yelled, raking his claws down Draco's underbelly.

I guess he can't see Adonaias, I thought. It made sense; Elysian had avoided meeting him directly before. The more I thought about it, the more I could see it; Elysian wanted a peek, but he didn't want to get caught doing the peeking. Adonaias likely knew that.

Before Raiya or I could respond to Elysian's call, Adonaias vanished, and we were left back in the center of the storm of wind and shadow.

I squeezed Raiya's hand. "It'll be alright," I told her, even as I was the one who more likely had to be told that.

"Right." She nodded. "Let's—"

"Augh!" We both flinched and stalled, as Elysian howled in pain behind us. Hands together, we turned to see Draco laying him out against a hard surface, kicking his head further into the crumbling earth.

Elysian stilled, and I felt my heart stop as Draco laughed.

He turned to us. "My brother always thought he would be better than me one day," he said. "I've waited centuries, millennia, to prove him wrong."

"Get up, Elysian!" I cried. I took a step toward him, but Raiya held me back.

"We need to stop Alküzor," she said.

I didn't really want to hear her words. It took me twice as long to process them.

Draco turned on us, his long, scaly body, still dripping with blood and dust, snaking around us in unholy excitement. "There's no way you'll win," he taunted us, striking forward and snapping his fangs at us.

Alküzor roared, and a long, shady tongue launched out of the vortex's opening.

Before I could respond, I heard Elysian stir from his position on the ground.

Elysian coughed, but crawled out to do battle. "I don't need to win," he said, as he faced Draco, "I just need to make sure you lose."

With that, Elysian launched himself at Draco once more, this time grabbing onto his neck. Elysian's nose snorted out fire and blood, as his eyes turned orange with pain and power.

He managed to wrestle Draco over to the void's opening. Raiya and I watched in horror as he dived in, the darkness encasing him and Draco, as they both roared and burned with new levels of pain.

"Elysian," I called. "Wait!"

Raiya was with me this time, as I leapt forward, casting myself into the foyer room of Hell.

☼15☼
Trial by Fire

I coughed and sputtered and gasped, as ash and soot flooded my vision and my throat. My wings fluttered around as much as they could, shielding me and Raiya from the worst of it.

"I'm supposed to follow your lead," Raiya called from beside me.

"Don't let go," I begged her. There was something about this place that made the idea of loneliness all the more terrifying, and I was terrified enough.

All of a sudden, I saw my dream again—the one that had haunted me since Draco revealed himself. I saw Raiya, alone and unsure, and sad because there was nothing left to feel.

I tightened my grip on her.

I was almost grateful for the distraction as a loud, monstrous groan gutted out behind us.

That was the moment I got my first really good look at Alküzor. He was a demon of fire and density, collecting the matter of the world and eating up Time's residue to keep the dreariness of his pride intact.

It was then that I realized Alküzor wasn't just in Hell; he *was* Hell.

Or at least part of it. The fires around us burned black, and any light we had was painfully obscured—clear enough to taunt us, perhaps, but foggy enough to lose us.

On the other side of me, I could hear Elysian and Draco still fighting it out, though if they were doing so with each other or not, I couldn't see.

I breathed in as deeply as I could without polluting my lungs beyond capacity, and then drew on my center of calm. In my one hand, I still clung to Raiya; in my other, I had my sword.

It was then, as I choked and struggled to remain strong, that I noticed I could see Draco's sword below us. It was as black and burnt as the devil's word, and I had to destroy it with the sword I had been given.

If I could do that, I realized, we would still need to hold off Alküzor and Draco until the hole was closed off, before leaving ourselves. It seemed like a lot of work, and a high-risk challenge, but it was the only way I could see to make things right.

We can do it. I know we can.

"Call your power," I instructed Raiya. "We're going to launch all we have here at Draco's sword."

"That'll close the barrier," Raiya said.

"Watch out," I called, as a stream of fire and energy flew all around us. I knew at once, from the different feel and look of it, Alküzor was attacking.

But Alküzor's power moved all around us, never touching us. I was about to make fun of him for having such a lousy aim when I realized Raiya and I were glowing with a protective shield.

Was it the joint power we shared, or had Adonaias given us one last gift of protection before we went into the oven of the earth?

Raiya shuddered beside me. "I don't think your idea is going to work."

"I know it's risky. We'll have to make a run for it," I said. "Although that's not the right verb for it."

"I'm sure Mrs. Night would commend you for realizing that," Raiya called back sarcastically. "What if we don't make it?"

"We can!" I argued.

"Since when are you such an optimist?"

"Well," I said, giving up, "we have to try."

Raiya sighed. "Alright. Just do it!"

At her words, I felt our power combine, coming together, mixing with our blood, running through our hearts and our hands. I felt as though we had created our own supernova of sorts, a binary star pairing, as we poured out our power to light up the darkness of the crushing void.

When I felt it had built up enough, I gazed downward.

I had a clear shot of Draco's sword.

Nothing was stopping me, and every ounce of power I possessed guided me. I tossed my sword downward, letting it slice through the scorching clouds and flames around us.

The moment my sword left my hand, Raiya and I unleashed our power together after it, as we both yelled—me in triumph, her in frustration, and all of it tied together with the most primal and fervent prayer for this to work.

By some miracle (poor choice of words at this point), my sword flew down and cut through Draco's sword. With my power and Raiya's following swiftly behind it, Draco's sword smashed, crackling into a million and a half tiny little pieces. The earth began to return, pushing back against the remaining intrusion. I could see my sword, cast into the dirt and dust of the weary world. Its power faded, and the sword darkened.

I knew, instantly, that its job was done.

Surrounding us, our power continued to spread out, shining a bright light of hope, like a star trapped inside the world finally breaking free. I almost had to wonder if the Star of Hope, whom I'd met a couple of Christmases ago, would come down with her fairylike Star babies and dance around it.

Alküzor didn't like it; he forced himself against us, trying to drown out the light with his own fire.

Raiya cried out in pain, as a tongue of fire snaked out and cut her arm. Her blood ran out, scorching Alküzor and making him fluster more of his darkened fire.

I felt her weaken next to me. "Are you alright?" I asked.

Her energy was low, and I saw her face run pale. Her emotions flickered out to me—there were traces of desperation, weariness, a resigned quality. But there was also an angry determination, and while I was glad she was still fighting, I felt fear tug at me.

"I'm fine," she insisted, showing nothing in her expression or tone that would've made me look twice.

She'll die if she keeps fighting.

I had to do something.

With my free hand, I reached over and drew her close to me. I kissed her, hoping fervently that it wouldn't be our last, even as I feared it would be.

Dante's words came back to me. *To release the Blood Flame, I had to die.*

Or at least, I had to pull my Soulfire out of my body. Which was more or less the scientific equivalent of dead, right?

"What are you doing?" Raiya asked. Fear was starting to crack through her mask.

"Hold your power as much as you can," I instructed her.

Using my free hand, I pressed into the mark on my wrist, hoping my power wouldn't harm her.

It wasn't the most graceful of motions, as I reached inside of my heart and tried to pull it out of me.

I saw my heart, the pure-white clouds of the confusion around me and my identity, and the bridge between my regular self and my supernatural self.

Since the last time I'd seen it, and the one time I tried to dismantle it, the connections between the two had been rectified and reinforced—two halves of my life that had been splintered and shattered, but like a part of my body, they were healing up the fissures, this time with more intention and appreciation.

Awe struck me all over again at the sight. Different memories, as they hung in crystal balls like the one Aleia had carried with her throughout her time on Earth.

I was tempted to take a closer look at some of them, but I shook my head. "Later, later," I promised myself.

At the center of my heart, I saw it—my Soulfire.

I came up to it, and held out my hands to receive it.

When I first saw them, I thought all of them were like tiny balls of fire and light. Looking at it now, I realized I was both right and wrong. It was a glowing force, a mishmash of separate things bound together—the integration of emotion and intellect, reality and possibility, reason and intuition, will and wish, all into a form that did not diminish nor enhance their individual power when they came together, even as it increased its value.

It really is amazing to think everyone has one of these! And they are all different, too.

Everyone had a Soulfire. Mine was further protected by my Starlight defender identity, the Starfire and the Starsoul, which wrapped around my essence like a ghost and allowed me to freely communicate with the Celestial Kingdom (assuming I would ever figure that one out).

Gazing at it, I saw the fire within the fire; some part of it was not my own, but another's, and that held everything together in perfect harmony.

I held onto the Soulfire. For a quick second, I saw a reflection of my former self staring out at me. "Time to be brave, Almeisan," I told myself. "But you can do it. It's for Raiya."

The reflection smiled back at me, a cynical smile on his face where I would've thought a happy one would reside. I frowned back at him, or me, I guess, as I called my self out of my self, back to the battlefield.

Later on, I would recall my other self's expression and wonder if he was trying to remind me that all power had its price.

☼

Instantly, I was back in the middle of the battle. But my Soulfire was out, and its light was shining in full force.

"You can't do this," Raiya warned me. "I won't let you die."

"That was the plan," I told her, feeling strangely stretched with my power before me. I'd had this feeling before, once, when Elektra managed to pull my Soulfire from my body. My vision slipped all the way around me, and I could see things in more dimensions. It was hard to describe the sensation, especially in a way that didn't sound like I was on drugs.

Her power to me increased as she no doubt sensed my discomfort.

"I know you're in pain," I said, "but we only need a few moments of power to keep Alküzor and Draco in this dimension."

"Just tell me what you need," she ordered. "I can handle it."

I didn't want to. I knew she was tired from our battles, and I was rapidly tiring too. But we had to do it. It was the only way to stop.

"Supernova time," I told her.

We exchanged careful glances, as I took hold of both of her hands. "After that, it'll be alright."

"Just like last time, right?" She gave me a small smile.

I grinned back. "Exactly."

And with that, the light burst out all around us. I closed my eyes against the rush, and for the moment, I felt the peace of protection, and then the forefront of the battle pushed against us.

I heard Raiya shouting, and I heard my own shout, as we came together.

My memory flashed against my mind, and I saw this same thing as before—Raiya on the other side of Time's power, her own supernova raging against an impossible barrier, and breaking free when I crashed into her.

Opening my eyes, I could see it all; I saw, for the briefest second, into the life of the eternal.

I barely fought off the darkness as it came for me, taking the last of my energy reserves. I pushed through for Raiya, keeping my hands in hers.

"Look," Raiya said, her voice as weary as I felt. "It's working."

The resulting light was too much for Alküzor. I caught a glimpse of the terror in his piercing green eyes, as he narrowed them and then turned and fled farther into the world's burning heart. For such a large and imposing figure, made of flaming fire, he sure darted away from the light quickly. Some of the opaque clouding went away with him, and I could finally breathe relatively normal once more.

"Awesome," Raiya whispered beside me, watching as the last of the light filtered back into our world as my Soulfire sank back into the chamber of my heart.

I felt like cheering. *I didn't die! The plan worked! It really worked!*

I had to wonder if Raiya didn't feel some of my joy and my excitement (and if I was going to get a tirade from her, since I tried something that almost killed me and tried to hide it from her). "We need to go."

I nodded. "We're not out of this yet."

"Right."

"Elysian," I called. "Time to go!"

Draco's head popped out of the bed of flames. His teeth snapped at my wingdings, and I cringed in pain.

"Stop it!" Raiya yelled, pulling out her bow. She wasn't able to let go of me to load it, so she used the edge of it to strike him across the jaw.

He reared back in pain, and then retaliated. Raiya brought up her bow to deflect it.

"Elysian!" I called. "Where are you?"

There was nothing.

"Elysian!" I called even louder, all while trying to dodge Draco's frequent snapping.

"I'm here," he said, "holding onto Draco's tail."

"We've got to go."

"Hey," he said. "I want to say I'm sorry."

"Sorry for what?" I asked. "Let's go."

"No. Not until you forgive me. For all the judging, and all the attitude, and all that."

"What are you talking about?" I glared at him, while Raiya managed to dodge another attack. Her bow shot out, catching Draco between the eyes.

"Do you forgive me?" Each word out of Elysian's mouth had a grating undertone, one that weirded me out. Normally, I think I would have been angered by it, but I was just desperate to leave. Draco's power on the earth was gone, and our only way out was closing fast.

"Of course I forgive you," I told him. "You're my friend."

"Really? Do you really mean it?"

"Yes!" I shook my head. "Now, come on. We've got to go!"

"No," Elysian told me. "You've got to go. I've got to protect you."

"What are you—"

It was only when I heard a different kind of snapping that I went still.

My gaze swiveled to Raiya's as her bow shattered by Draco's biting power. Her mouth dropped open in pained surprise, and her eyes glazed over in disbelief.

The broken pieces of her bow sparkled, before the river of fire around us swept them up, flushing them further down into the heart of fiery darkness. I felt the last of her supernatural power break inside of her.

"Raiya!"

I was surprised that I wasn't the only one who called out her name.

I narrowed my eyes at Draco. I only stopped my attack because, for the smallest, most minute second of time, I'd heard him: Grandpa Odd. The old man's eyes pierced through the redness of Draco the dragon's.

Justice will be his undoing.

The words echoed in my mind.

Before I could make sense of it, he backed away. Raiya's tears began to slip free, and Draco allowed Elysian to grab onto him once more. I watched, unable to say anything

Immediately, I felt a pull on my own shoulder, as if my body remembered Adonaias' commands better than my brain did at that moment.

The vortex's power was gone, and the momentary, makeshift entrance to the realm inside the earth was closing.

I barely thought anything, as I pushed myself out of the hole and then turned to Raiya.

"Come on," I called back to her as I pulled her up.

"Let me go," she said.

"What? No!" I gripped her hand even harder in mine.

"My bow broke," she said.

"And I had to rip my Soulfire out of my body," I snapped back. "And Elysian made sure that the world is being protected from Draco by sacrificing himself! We've all had losses. We still have things we need to do."

"My power is gone," Raiya tried again. "My mission is over."

"Adonaias told us not to let go of each other," I yelled back.

"But we finished what we had to do."

"You'll get a new mission, then," I said. "I still need you."

"But—"

"You promised!" I shouted. "You promised me you would live for me."

She sighed. "Okay. You're right. Pull me up."

Really? I have to cajole her into staying alive? I groaned inwardly as I hoisted her out of the other realm. I felt bad that she lost her bow. I would feel lost, too, if I wasn't able to use my sword to help us get out of the vortex.

The opening between the two realms closed just seconds after we cleared it.

And then it was over.

A numbness fell over me, and even Raiya's presence beside me was hard to grasp onto as we stared at the sight before us.

The vortex had pushed a crater into the ground, much larger than the one the meteorite had. In the center of it, still stuck in the ground, was my sword.

We made it out just in time. The vortex disappeared, the skies cleared up, and Time's power—familiar enough to notice, but subtle enough to miss—resumed.

I felt the shield of protection, the one I'd felt so surely when we were in the midst of trouble, disappear. Adonaias' gift had been given and had been used for its intended task.

"Well done, good and faithful one."

The words whispered out to me from nowhere, but there was no mistaking the reality of them.

THE STARLIGHT CHRONICLES

☼16☼
Battle of the Heart

I grappled with the end of the battle. I was glad I had done a good job, but I was still sad at saying good-bye to Elysian.

Raiya was breathing hard on the ground next to me, as the vortex died, and my sword remained stuck in the ground, in the center of the large crater where Rosemont used to be.

The night resumed quietly; I couldn't tell if it had begun while my sword struck Draco's, or if it just resumed as we'd shut the wormhole into Alküzor's realm.

I pulled Raiya over next to me. We were both heaving, laboring for breath, and covered in sweat. But neither stopped me from reaching over and peeling some of her hair away from her face, and kissing her.

Beneath all the sweat and tears and blood and dirt, I could still taste her. It was the most bittersweet kiss of my life, I decided, half in jest.

"It's over," I whispered.

"We did it," she said, her voice incredulous at the realization that we'd survived, and we'd won.

In the distance, I could hear fire alarms going off, cars honking, and the other sounds of rescue teams, as they went around to the different parts of the city that had fallen apart.

I stood up. "Come on," I said, tugging at her. "Let's get out of this hole. It's making me uncomfortable."

Raiya coughed and struggled up the hill, but I held onto her, moving her forward. We reached the top of the crater and fell onto the grass.

I breathed in the smell of the grass and wondered at it. I knew I'd been so close to never seeing this world again. There was no taking things for granted. Not anymore.

Especially since victory had come at a high cost.

"Elysian didn't make it," I said, barely hearing myself say the words. I turned to see Raiya, as she wore the same stricken look of shock on her face I'd seen when her bow broke.

I turned away and stared at the ground, hoping for a miracle. Hoping that Elysian would burst out of the ground and then chide me for worrying in the first place.

And then we could argue all night long about who got what end of the bed and which blankets smelled like human versus the ones that smelled like dragon.

Then I heard a coughing sound. "Raiya?" I asked. "Are you alright?"

She gasped in pain as she doubled over, grabbing at her chest.

"What's wrong?" I cried. "What's happening?" I caught her and held her up, cradling her against me.

"Hamilton," she whispered.

I kneeled down onto the ground, lying her carefully on her back, using my knees as a pillow. "What? What is it?" I asked, checking her temperature. I saw that her wound, the one on her arm that Draco had inflicted, was still bleeding out.

Has something happened to her heart? I wondered. A warning bell rang out in my head. She'd told me before, if I lost too much blood, there wouldn't be anything she could do for me. It was likely true for her, too.

Weakly, Raiya pulled me close to her. "I'll be waiting for you," she said, before her eyes closed.

She went limp before I could ask her what she meant.

I felt her cheeks as they went soft, and I felt her pulse as it went weak; I watched as the Emblem of the Prince, the mark we shared under his banner, disappear from her wrist.

"Raiya?" I cupped her cheek and held her close, giving her a desperate kiss, as my last attempts at coherency failed me.

The image of her bow snapping shot through my mind. Was her heart truly broken at last?

"Come back," I begged her, my voice suddenly thick and scratchy. I placed my hand over her silent heart, reaching out to her in the only way I could. "Come back to me."

Nothing happened. Nothing changed.

"Adonaias!" I yelled. "Adonaias, help me! Please, we need your help … "

I saw him appear before us. He said nothing, only stretched out his arms. The white of his tunic fluttered in the wind of my world as he waited for me to come rushing to him.

"She needs your help," I tried to explain to him. "She's … "

I couldn't say it. I wouldn't say it.

"You need to help her," I repeated, when he didn't move.

His eyes glittered as they looked into mine.

It was at that moment that I realized he wasn't going to help.

"No," I shouted. "No, get away. You can't have her!"

He didn't move. His arms were still outstretched, waiting for me.

"No!" I hugged Raiya's limp form to my chest even more tightly. "No, don't. Please don't."

Nothing.

"You can't have her! If she dies, you can't have me, either!" I shouted, hardly realizing my sadness and despair were quickly morphing into anger and bitterness. "I can't live without her—huh?"

I was surprised to feel his hand on my shoulder. Peace settled on me, and I could feel Raiya's soul resting peacefully, too. I looked up into Adonaias' eyes, their light piercing through my thick veil of tears.

"I make all things new," he said, softly and surely.

It was a funny choice of words for the guy. Especially as the shallow peace Adonaias had brought me was just that— shallow. The cloak of protection I'd felt before whisked away, transforming into an insubstantial shadow.

Adonaias disappeared as I turned from him, and I told myself very certainly that I did not miss him.

I cuddled Raiya into my body as I tried to move her. *I have to find a hospital,* I thought. It wasn't that far away. I could carry her. Couldn't I?

I felt weak and numb as I tried to lift her. My power was dwindling, my energy was being depleted, and fast.

"Somebody, help!" I called, resuming my search for help.

Time passed, and my voice became cracked as I continued to cry out, calling out for help, any help at all. I eventually remembered health class, and tried CPR. I was screaming before long.

I watched the fires of the feather in her hair, the one I gave her, as it slipped away into ash. I said plenty of words, and saw other things, but I couldn't be entirely sure of them, since my eyes were running over with water.

I thought I saw some emergency medics heading our way. I saw people moving, and I couldn't do anything about it as I sat there in the middle of the grass, finally overwhelmed and crushed by life's expectations.

The last thing I felt, before I closed my eyes, was the soft touch of snowflakes on my skin. And then, all I felt was the familiar sting of lightning as it tasered through my body.

I woke up, some unknown amount of time later, in the hospital.

I was in one of those pitiful little rooms, where it looked more like a storage room for the older models of medical tech. I was no longer transformed, but I had on a hospital gown. I was hooked up to an IV, and I felt as though I'd been poked and prodded in places I didn't want to think about.

The smell was the worst part, but, considering I had some idea of what true pain felt like, I knew I could ignore it.

There were some things I couldn't ignore, two of which struck me right away. The first thing I saw was that the Emblem of the Prince was gone.

My mission was over. I couldn't transform into Wingdinger anymore. I assumed, anyway; I didn't bother to try, and I knew I wasn't going to.

The second thing I noticed was that my eyes were still crinkly and blotchy. Remembering what happened took a toll on me I never really measured.

My nose prickled with pressure, and my sinuses were ready to explode. I felt the same amount of fear and helplessness as I had before the battle.

This time, Adonaias didn't come. I felt his presence, but I didn't see him, didn't hear him, didn't want him. Instead, I pressed back into my pillow, trying to push back the rest of my tears.

Once more it hit me, that Adonaias just didn't fit in with normal suffering. What did he know of losing someone like Raiya? What did he know of pain like mine?

My mark was gone.

My sword was gone.

Elysian was gone.

Raiya was gone.

I wished I was gone, too.

I guess I went to sleep again, because I woke up again, still unsure how much time had passed. I felt numb to all power, all forces. I didn't care that it was dark, I didn't care that it was cold. I didn't even care I hadn't eaten.

Even Mark's presence wasn't enough to make me worried.

"Hamilton," he said, and not for the first time, my name sounded completely alien to me. "You're awake."

I looked over at him. I wanted to scream, *"Congratulations on your superb observations skills, Captain Obvious!"*

But I held myself back. Just like I held my tears back. I breathed in, sharply and deeply, trying to recall I had to live, even if I didn't really want to.

"You've been in here for a couple of days," Mark told me, answering at least one of the questions I might've asked if it mattered to me anymore. "The reports have gone out, saying that you and some others were caught up in a surprise gas leak near the old Rosemont School that the repair crew missed."

I said nothing. Mark would need to go away soon enough. I doubted he was here during his off-hours. I was too old to remember if he had ever had any off-hours that he sought to really spend time with me.

Losing my will to live, even if my body insisted on dragging me through it, while death seemed unwilling to let me die, didn't seem like something Mark would change for.

Minutes passed before he spoke again.

"I don't suppose you really care about the cover story," he said.

I looked back over at him, still silent.

"Dante brought you here," he said, "after everything."

Everything.

What a quaint manner in which to discuss the death of not only Raiya, but Elysian, too. It was also a way to diminish their effort to stop Draco, to stop Alküzor, to stop the destruction of the world and the universe and *everything.*

"He asked me to find a private room for you," Mark went on. "He thought it would be best to keep you here until you recovered."

If I recover.

"You were pretty beat up," Mark continued. "You had a large laceration on your arm, and several other scrapes. You were in a state of shock when you woke up the first time. We kept you down for a little bit, but we stopped the morphine drip for now.

"If you're worried about your identity, don't be. Dante and I were able to cover it up."

I can't believe he thinks I would worry about that now, of all times.

As Mark continued to tell me of how he had been on duty when the attack happened, and how he'd been called right after surgery, I took the time to glance back down at my wrist.

The mark was still gone. I ran my fingers over my wrist, my hands shaking slightly. I didn't want the mark any longer; I felt used, abused, and discarded. I felt like I didn't matter at all.

How could I? Life didn't matter anymore, therefore it was ridiculous to even think I mattered.

"Your mother is hoping that you will be able to get back to school soon," Mark said. "They've talked to us about delaying your AP exams until you've been through physical therapy. You might need it for your arm, since the cut was so deep," he explained.

Again, why would I care about this?

Mark eventually dropped off into silence. I felt relieved. I didn't want the responsibility of keeping the pretense of caring. I wasn't really paying much attention, anyway, although I managed to give a silent, half-hearted, "yay," as he told me Cheryl had let Ayako go. As much as I appreciated her kindness, her culinary tastes could easily go to hell.

Which was where I was. Alone, alone, and more alone. I was living through hell.

Finally, Mark sighed. He looked over at me somberly, like he was going to say something else (I prepared myself for the inevitable cringe), when his beeper went off.

He was being called back into a heart surgery.

"Well," Mark said, "I've got to go." He rose from his chair.

I was surprised when he leaned over and kissed my forehead. He hugged me, slightly, so as not to disturb my bandages.

"I love you, son," he said, quietly but firmly, and in his own doctor/father way, I knew he was telling me to keep holding

THE STARLIGHT CHRONICLES

on. If I couldn't move on, if I couldn't continue on, the best thing was not to fall away.

He had only taken a step away from me when I spoke.

"What happened to Starry Knight?"

He jumped at my voice—I couldn't blame him, I sounded like some kind of monster—before he turned around.

"Please," he said, "please, don't ask me that."

I frowned. Instantly, I sat up as straight as I could. "Tell me," I commanded, hoping that he would realize *not* knowing was the greater pain.

I felt a tingle of fear when Mark narrowed his eyes at me, which he had never done quite so horrifically. "I can't give you the answers you're looking for. Please don't ask anything of me again, Hamilton."

And then he walked out the door after adjusting the morphine tap.

It was almost welcoming to feel the rush of numbness replaced by the desire to sleep.

Some part of me, shocked at both ends of my father's behavior, fully expected to die, even as he wanted me to survive.

When I did wake up, and I mean for real wake up, and not just to be forced to eat or change clothes or bathe, I found Dante staring down at me.

Mustering up what strength I could, hoping I wouldn't end up slurring my words, I spoke up.

"What happened to Starry Knight?"

To his credit, Dante didn't try to distract me from the truth of the matter.

"She died."

He told me, so simply. I wondered if he would have answered me in a similar manner if I'd asked what was for dinner.

My chest felt swollen and bruised, as those simple words killed me all over again.

"Do you want to know the specifics?" Dante asked, making me wonder if he wasn't getting some kind of sick pleasure out of my absolute misery.

I nodded.

"We reached you after we were able to move again," he said. "We didn't realize all that had happened, but we saw you both come up from the crater. You were both struggling, so we got the medical kits ready."

I nodded. "I remember," I admitted quietly.

"Then you'll remember that you were inconsolable at the time," Dante said. "We had to put you down."

The fire of being tasered ran through my memory. I nodded.

"We brought you both here. We tried to save her. We didn't."

"What happened to her?" I asked.

"Your father warned her before about her heart," Dante said. "She had an irregular heart. Mark even put her on the transplant list several years ago."

She never mentioned that.

But I waved the thought away a second later. Until recently, she'd planned to die fighting the Sinisters and their cronies.

"We moved her into surgery," Dante continued, "to see if we could restart her heart. Nothing worked. When we cut into her body, water came out along with blood."

I remembered that description from somewhere else. "Her heart exploded."

"Yes."

Bitter laughter echoed from the depths inside of me. "Well," I said, "it wouldn't be the first time she left me that way."

Dante said nothing about that. He changed the subject. A wise move, and one that I could appreciate, despite the fact that I still half-hated him.

"You've been placed under special care," he said, "and your parents are understandably upset, but as you can see, they are still working. Some people grieve with work, you know."

My parents have been "grieving" with work for a lot longer than the last three days.

"There was a lot of damage down to the area where the battle was," he said. "There were also other places where the explosions caused damage, including Shoreside Park, and Lakeview Observatory. No one was seriously hurt. Maybe that was a miracle."

His choice of words burned me, inflicting another round of wounds on me.

Adonaias had failed to save Raiya. He'd tried to comfort me, too, to make it worse.

Dante was still talking, taking my silence as a sign I wished for him to continue. I didn't, but I let him.

I was tired, and I felt numb, and I wanted nothing to do with anything anymore.

Maybe, if I was silent long enough, he would give me a reason to keep on fighting. Or maybe he would bore me to death and I would be saved that way.

Salvation through damnation, I thought bitterly.

He only spiked my interest, briefly, when he mentioned Mikey wanted to come visit me.

"Why?" I spat. "So he can rub everything in my face?"

"I told him no," Dante said, "if it makes you feel better."

I glared at him, my temper flaring. *Only death will make me feel better.*

"If you want him to visit, I'll be happy to send him the message," Dante said. "But that is something up to you, and I would not take that choice away for anyone's sake, not even my son's."

I had to stop myself from saying that it was not a surprise to him, since Dante had the gall to leave Mikey and his family in the first place. He never seemed to have trouble disappointing his family.

"Where is Starry Knight now?" I asked. "Can I ... can I at least see her ... "

In response to my question, Dante pushed the morphine tab. My IV drip began to increase, and I felt woozy only seconds later.

"You'd better hope I don't get addicted to that stuff," I murmured.

"Let's hope for the hospital's sake," Dante corrected me. "But I believe it's better for you to hear this now, when you're unable to lose it again: Starry Knight gave all she had to protect you and this world."

I felt even more numb, and not just from the morphine. I barely heard the rest of Dante's speech as he told me that even though they have to deny the supernatural aspect of this situation to the public, citing that political power is best left out of the hands of those who would seek divine right to rule, or abuse the notions which have destroyed the past civilizations, he would always consider Starry Knight a true heroine.

"But she is gone from your life, Hamilton, and there is no escaping it," he finished.

And then the darkness, the emptiness which had embraced me before, welcomed me back with mocking arms.

I had been blinded by the light inside of me, by the light of creation and power, an unparalleled spirited fire for goodness, justice, love, and mercy, too awesome to describe or even say without trembling.

But I found I was blindsided by Raiya's absence. The light inside of me was gone, and so was she. I didn't know how awful the vengeance of darkness and despair could be before that moment. But then that moment came, and I knew and it was enough for my own heart to die a star's death, and cave in on itself till there was nothing left, with the fullness of my emptiness crushing me from all sides with unimaginable strength and power.

It had to have been grace that saved me, because I could not, would not, have saved myself.

When I woke up again, I saw a shadow shifting outside the door.

"Well, come in," I called out. "I can see you."

I wasn't that surprised to see Mikey walk through the door.

"So," he said tentatively, "you're awake."

I frowned at him.

"You've looked worse," he said. He was obviously trying to cheer me up, and possibly avoid apologizing to me. I wasn't up for either one.

"What are you doing here?" I grumbled. "I thought Dante told you to stay away."

"Well, he also told my mother they would be together until death do they part," he retorted.

"I thought he was your buddy now."

"He never really was," Mikey gave me a small smile. "I know I said that he was before, but I was just using him to see if he could help Gwen."

I cocked an eyebrow at him. Mikey didn't seem that smart.

He blushed, and I was surprised as I realized I could still read people's emotions. They were still responding to my scrutiny in color, too, just as before. His embarrassment and humiliation leapt off him as he tried to conceal it.

"Well, anyway, he told me that he's got a new project, and so he's leaving again," Mikey admitted.

"Where is he going?" I asked, surprised. Dante told me before that Otherworld had been let go, but SWORD was still an active force in Apollo City. Was it possible that they had just come to stop Draco and the Sinisters, and all them, really?

"I don't know," Mikey said. "I hope far away though. For you more than me," he added. "I know you probably don't want to see him right now."

I snorted. "If I ever see him again, it'll be too soon. He told me that I had to die to save the city, you know."

"He did?"

"Yeah."

"Did you?"

Not well enough, I thought. But instead, I shrugged. "No."

"Well, that's good." Mikey smiled at me, but I just glared at him.

"I get that it's your turn to be upset," he said. "I wanted to say I was sorry for everything, and I hope we can still be friends."

"Friends don't normally have the issues we do," I retorted. But I remembered what Raiya said before, about having relationships tested, and as I shoved her further from my mind, I relented. "But I know you'll need the help graduating on time."

"Yeah, no kidding," Mikey agreed. He seemed a bit happier. I hoped it wasn't just because I implied I'd help him with his homework.

THE STARLIGHT CHRONICLES

"So," he said, "when are you getting out of here?"

"I don't know," I told him truthfully. Part of me didn't want to leave. That meant I would have to go on living, and there was no reason to do that now that Raiya was gone. The hospital had always been this depressing place of death for me. Now, it was a depressing place of stillness, where I couldn't go back, and I couldn't go forward, almost like a purgatory that smelled like cleaning alcohol.

"Can you move?" he asked.

"I suppose. Why?" I asked. I wondered if he was going to make me go down to the cafeteria with him. It was the sort of thing I could expect from Mikey.

So I was surprised when he said, "I thought you'd want to go and see Gwen and the others," he said. "They've all woken up."

"I don't know … "

He tugged at my arm, the one with the large gash in it from Raiya's arrow, and I winced in pain. He didn't notice. "Come on. It'll be good for you. I've already talked with her some. She's just down a few floors."

I didn't care, I reminded myself, but Mikey did, and shrugging him off would likely cause me more pain, physically.

So we went down to the room, arriving just as Gwen was getting checked out.

I noticed that her auburn hair was much longer, and seemed to be darker closer to the roots.

I wished I could say that she was happy to see me.

The moment she saw me, her honey-colored eyes darkened. "Well, if it isn't my least favorite ex."

I gave Mikey a look that said, "I told you so," before turning back to Gwen. "Hi, Gwen."

"You have some nerve, showing up here," she muttered. "You let me get captured, and you didn't save me."

I didn't bother to tell her that technically, I *did* save her, and everyone else, too. I just let her vent. Her words couldn't hurt me anymore, and thankfully, since Dante had mentioned he was releasing a statement to say that both Starry Knight and Wingdinger died in the blast that occurred, she couldn't blackmail me anymore.

I considered it the truth anyway.

As I listened to Gwen as she continued to ramble on, and I watched Mikey as he tried to get her to stop, I realized something uncomfortably inconvenient.

I was not the only one was who in pain. I was still pretty sure that I was the only one who would be in pain for the rest of his life, though.

So I decided to try to help Gwen.

I tapped her on the shoulder. "What is it that you're really angry with me over, Gwen?" I asked. "I mean, really?"

It's hard to downplay getting your soul sucked out by a demonic being bent on destroying the universe, but I managed.

"I'm angry that you didn't love me," Gwen finally admitted, as fresh tears swelled up in her eyes. "I would've loved you forever, if you'd only have let me."

I'm glad I didn't.

I didn't tell her that, though.

"I'm sorry," I said. That's all I could say. I didn't tell her it was her fault (even though it mostly was) and I didn't tell her that I loved someone else more (which was definitely true) and I didn't tell her that I wanted to be friends or fix anything (which would have been brutal, to be honest).

So I let her know that I was worthy of her hatred more than her love, and I let Mikey take over when she needed a shoulder to cry on.

As I walked out of the room, I turned back to look at them. As terrible as the whole situation was, I wasn't jealous of them. I wished I had Raiya, but I didn't. Some part of me knew that I would have to go on without her. But all of me knew that Mikey and Gwen deserved to get their chance to be together, and I hoped that it made them happy. I silently wished them all the best as the door swung shut behind me.

☼17☼
The Real Battle

The following months were speckled with waking moments, where I found myself back to acting like myself.

Grieving privately, I was ashamed that I had been found to be a fool. Who was I, to think I was anything or anyone important, or that my life would leave a mark on the world in which I lived? Accomplishments I may have had, but they were nothing in the light of eternity. Actually, I don't think nothing is the best word to describe it. They were more like eclipses, shadowing the real meaning of true meaning from me even further, removing me from the truth found only in choosing to face the stark, unfiltered starlight.

There were a million, million times when I wished that the meteorite had just damaged the city when it'd struck. Easily half of those were wished after Raiya was gone.

Only once, after high school was over, did I go out to the ruins of Rosemont Academy, where my sword remained stuck. A demolition group was working on the area, trying to turn it into an underground mall. My sword would eventually become its centerpiece. I figured it was appropriate, in many ways. The meteorite had struck into the heart of the earth, unleashing the enemy's ambitions. My sword, and the power behind it, had stopped it.

My friends never said anything much to me about that year of school, and if they did, it was silenced it quickly enough.

Mikey managed to prove somewhat useful in the end, acting as my advocate more than he had to. I could tell he was never entirely certain of my position on his position in my life, but, true to his nature and our habits, he clung to me like a second shadow.

Things changed a bit when he got a swim scholarship to Ohio State. Coach Uzzy was so proud of him.

Gwen was even more hesitant, even more terrified of me. There was one time between the moments and months of time continuing where she looked at me, caught my eye, and tried to say something.

She was walking toward the auditorium of the school, no doubt going to see Mr. Lockard, the old drama teacher, who had also been awakened from his soulless state, as he came to work beside Ms. Carmichael on the school play, *Pippin*.

Our eyes met more by accident, and in them, I could see she wanted to ask me for something. But it was something I was not sure I wanted to give her, so when I turned away, that seemed to be the end of it. She shied away from me for the rest of the year, and several years after that as well.

Before I knew it, the school year was over. Soon after, summer was over.

My sabbatical from work was over. I went back, finishing up another month with Assistant Mayor Dunbooke and then finishing out the rest of Mayor Mills' tenure. I never called him Stefano again, and I decided I never wanted to run for mayor.

My mother's business took off.

My dad's work stayed about the same.

They made arrangements for me to get a car for college after I got my license.

I joined the football team again, much to Jason's happiness, especially since I made good on my promise, and he was given the quarterback position.

Samantha Carter, who had been one of the more annoying persons of interest during my high school years, was crowned homecoming queen. I was playing during the game, but when I got the chance, I came up to her, smiled, and congratulated her. It seemed like a nice thing for her, especially after all the time she'd been stuck in the sleeping sickness coma.

I also congratulated the homecoming king—her boyfriend, Guy Fitch.

Some part of me was very happy that they'd grown into their own, happy that they'd gotten something they'd wished for and wanted for so long. Even if I couldn't be happy for myself, I was happy for them.

I got my SAT scores back. 2394. I'd missed a couple of questions on the English section.

I entered into Apollo City College's dual enrollment program. In addition to some CLEP exams, I had sixty credits ready to transfer by the time the University of Pittsburgh accepted me, and a 4.2 GPA.

I broke four of my previous swim records.

I skipped prom the following year. Instead, I went on a "vacation" with my mom instead, as she negotiated some contracts for some company in the Czech Republic.

I was able to keep my title of "Tetris King." Once high school ended, I never picked my Game Pac up again.

Nothing big. Nothing grand. It was a normal life, just the one I wanted, and I hated most of it.

☼18☼
Martha

Time continued to pass, even if my pain did not.

Even my body seemed to get the message. The golden halo effect, which had clung to me in my prime superhero days, dimmed and eventually disappeared. Even my blondish hair faded back to brown, and even seemed to get darker, slowly slipping away from me as I slipped back into the "real world."

Despite my "normal" life, I had some more surprises coming at me, as if pain demanded that it be a forever part of that "normal" adage.

First, Mrs. Smithe retired at the end of my 11th grade year.

As I walked down the halls, headed for my locker at the end of the day, she pulled me aside.

We didn't say a word as we walked into her half-empty classroom. But the moment the door shut, and the rest of the world was shut out, she told me the truth.

She was leaving me, too.

"What? Why?!" Her admission finally allowed me to give a proper vent to some of the suffocating grief I carried.

"Do you know why I told you I worked for SWORD before?" she asked.

"No." I snorted. "I don't."

"I told you," she said, "because I know what it is like to be without hope. I know what it is like to lose the people you love most, and have nothing left."

"Why are you telling me this now?" I balked.

"Because time and death are not permanent things," Martha said. "Not in the way that you think, anyway. Remember what I told you before? Your life is not about you. There must be something greater."

I watched her as she started slapping books and papers into a small box on her desk.

"Raiya's gone," I choked out, barely able to say her name. I found that it was much easier to pretend I was getting better if I didn't think about her. "I don't have anything greater."

"Her love is still real," Martha reminded me gently. "For her sake, find something greater."

I thought about Adonaias, about doing the right thing. Starlight Warrior duty was no longer an option, but even if it had been, I would've rejected it, just as I rejected Adonaias.

Rather than tell Martha the truth, I shrugged. "I don't know what it is yet."

"Extraordinary things come from ordinary places," she said. "You might just find something."

"What did you find?" I asked. "After SWORD killed your husband and son?"

I didn't mean to be mean about it, but my voice had a hard edge, one I knew was only half-intentional.

Martha came over to me and gave me a hug. It was awkward and tense, but strangely comforting in its stiffness. I could feel Martha's bony back and, despite her small frame, I felt the strength inside of her and her heart.

"I didn't find anything," she told me. "*I* was the one who was found."

Her cryptic remark made me jerk away. I was done with the pseudo-intellectual-spiritual-emotional crap. From that moment on, I only wanted to concern myself with what I could see and what I could touch and what I could understand.

"Thanks," I muttered, trying to hide my hurt. "I'll keep that in mind."

"See that you do," Martha said. "I expect law school will give you plenty to think about."

"You heard I got accepted to Pitt?"

"Of course." She gave me a small smile. "Your mother's very proud. She sent me a thank you note for preparing you."

"I'm surprised."

"I'm not." Martha picked up her coffee cup. "No one who knows you well would have second-guessed you."

I nodded. "Thanks." I didn't know what else to say.

"You'll do well in college, too," Martha said. "I know you will."

I nodded.

"Maybe we'll see each other again."

"Why?" I asked. "Are you going to go teach law or something in Pittsburg?"

"No." She grinned this time. "I'm retiring from teaching, and I'm going to go back to law school myself."

"I thought you already had your degree in law."

"Well, yes," she said, "but it's always been a dream of mine to go into practice. I need some more continuing education for that."

"Why are you going now?"

She glanced up at me. "Hamilton," she said, "there is a proper time for everything. I can't teach you any further, and I've reached my work requirement for my teacher's pension. For the moment, SWORD is leaving the city, and I have decided to leave, too. The time has come for me to move on."

I nodded again, more slowly this time. There was something to be said for timing, and I knew there was especially a time for retirement. If you can get one without the money worries, it was a good thing.

Reaching out, I took her hand. "Well," I said, "maybe I'll see you around Pitt, then."

"I've been accepted into Duquesne," she said. "But I'll be around in the city if you need a friend."

"A friend?" I asked, smiling for the first time in what seemed like a long time. I felt like an ancient old man, whose face was sunburned into submission, only to feel it crinkle and crack by the force of a miracle.

"Yes. I'm retiring, and you'll be eighteen next year." She sighed. "I suppose you can call me Martha now." She glanced at me over her thick-rimmed glasses. "Officially."

Shock, along with warmth, struck me in the heart, briefly breaking through the numbness that had settled in me in the last few weeks.

"Thank you," I finally replied, my voice soft.

Martha took my hand and squeezed it affectionately. "Now, skedaddle," she said. "I've got to finish cleaning out my room for the new teacher."

On some level, I knew, or at least I believed, that it would be the last time I saw her. Certainly, it would be the last time I left her classroom.

It was a moment that, like the previous moments of pain, should have broken me.

And maybe it did.

As I left her classroom, I felt the last of my teenage innocence slip away. I had worked all my life in classrooms, only to find that the real world didn't let you keep your troubles in nice, neat compartments. I'd known this before, but never realized until I walked out, full of certainty of Martha's approval, how uncertain life suddenly seemed. I was grateful for that—that small, unchanging element of life, as the rest of it all rocked around me, moved by the earthquakes of the moments and the shifting sands of the seconds.

As that chapter of my childhood closed, I felt a new one begin, one where weakness slumbered on, strength swiftly stirred.

For the moment—that moment, at least—I was comforted. I was not better, I was not unburdened, I was not past my pain. But I was comforted, and it strengthened me. It was enough to get me to the next moment, and the moment after that, and the next one after that.

It took me a lot longer to realize I could survive, and it took me much longer to realize I could even be happy again, and longer still to believe it was okay to be happy again.

THE STARLIGHT CHRONICLES

☼19☼
Good-bye

Saying good-bye to Martha wasn't the worst, surprisingly.

Of course, I didn't think about it at the time, but leaving in general was just the worst.

I blocked out everything I had of Raiya—from our memories together to the places she lived, worked, and dreamed—and left it all, all for my own desired comfort, rather than facing the uncomfortable truths I left behind.

Still, saying good-bye to Martha was like ripping the flesh off just over my heart.

Leaving my parents behind proved to be more easy and more difficult than I expected. I don't think I ever officially said good-bye to them. In the first weeks of summer break, something changed between us.

Cheryl busied herself with her work and her new firm, but stopped working overtime. She was home when I came home from work, and she was home when I came home from school after it started up at the end of summer. I can't remember a time in my life where she deliberately sought to give me more attention, and paid much more attention to what I wanted and what I needed. And me, finally receiving her attentions without working hard or trying to please her, or even without trying to tick her off, found that her love was a very small something I could learn to depend on in a world where more of myself had disappeared.

She even gave up the weird diets.

Mark, in comparison, began ignoring me and avoiding me. He said barely anything to me over the next several months. He was there, and he did things for me, but his forlorn detachment was enough to cause a sense of relief when I finally got ready to head off to college the next summer, starting a semester earlier than originally intended. I think that the handshake he gave me as I headed out the door settled something of whatever was bothering him about me, but I didn't know for sure.

I gave him a smile, regardless, because I knew as much as my heart was broken, he had been trusted and burdened with my true identity for longer than I had known, and he had protected me as best as he could. Some people would think that was expected of a doctor, or a parent, but I knew just how hard it really was to put yourself before any other person, even if you did love them. It is something that, if expected, becomes selfish and destructive.

No, my parents weren't hard to leave.

It was Rachel who was perhaps the hardest to say good-bye to.

When I walked into her café for the last time, the place where I had called my second home for the majority of my high school years, her eyes met mine and immediately sparkled with tears.

"Hamilton."

I was a little surprised she recognized me. I didn't go back to the café until I knew it was time to say good-bye for forever. "Hi, Rachel."

She tried to smile, to play it off, but it was Letty who really saved her from losing it.

"Just get it over with," Letty said. "You'll feel better."

"Mom!" Rachel gaped at her.

"What? It's true."

"I can't believe you're being so rude."

"Oh, well, dear. Life goes on," she scoffed, before lighting up a cigarette. Rachel, for once, did not stop her. Instead, she sat down, slumped over, and closed her eyes.

When she opened them, she thanked me, for everything, and that was that. There was so much unsaid but unable to be said, and so much we knew just couldn't be said. Saying some of those things would have ended something inside of us, and I had little enough left to go on. Rachel didn't look like she had the gumption for it, either, so we said, "See you soon," and "Keep in touch," and "Thanks," and that was it.

I did not even ask for a doggie bag.

Letty was, I suppose, trying to be helpful in her own way, but I think she wasn't completely right. Time goes on, the world goes on, and even life may go on, but it doesn't mean living goes on.

So I sat there, on the train, with my bags packed along with the pieces of my heart. A new chapter of my life was beginning. Or maybe it was ending, or both. Or maybe even neither. I didn't know.

I am a lawyer at heart, and as I saw it, there was a very big distinction between beginning and ending that started with hope and ended with expectation.

Thinking of endings made me think of my graduation day, of the speech I gave as valedictorian. I had somehow managed to find a speech inside of me devoid of several important memories, but still it managed to reveal more of myself than I ever could have guessed. My twelfth grade English teacher, Mrs. Runsallus, painstakingly prodded me to get it done and finished.

I remember making my speech. But rather than reading through the one I'd written, I made a new speech up, talking about how small things were great things, and how ordinary things became extraordinary, all thanks to life and love and other stuff that I thought sounded good. (This is the part that, should Hollywood ever get the rights to make a movie about me, they will have to make up. In all fairness, I was doing that, too, so I figured it would even out in the end.)

I didn't mention Raiya.

Maybe some part of me was trying to make up for never giving Raiya the speech she deserved. I was doing this, of course, in typical grief-stricken illogical fashion, by trying to pretend I'd never met her.

A wind had whipped by, scattering the music of heaven past me, and I found the first sparkle of hope as I looked down at my scattered speech papers, only to see the barest hint of a springtime violet anchored to the summer dirt. I picked it up, and then I heard it.

"I'll be waiting for you."

I heard the words, and nothing happened.

Nothing happened. Nothing.

It was a moment that breaks you or builds you, and you have the choice to decide which.

Later on, I knew, as the train left Apollo City, beginning its hustle toward Pittsburgh, pulling past the buildings of the city of my birth and childhood, past the places remembered, places forgotten, the foreign and the familiar, all the things which had made me who I was and promised to remain in me as I became something more … I knew I hadn't made up my mind just yet.

THE STARLIGHT CHRONICLES

THE STARLIGHT CHRONICLES

C. S. Johnson is the award-winning, genre-hopping author of several novels, including sci-fi and fantasy adventures such as *The Starlight Chronicles* series, the *Once Upon a Princess* saga, and the *Divine Space Pirates* trilogy. With a gift for sarcasm and an apologetic heart, she currently lives in Atlanta with her family.

AUTHOR'S NOTE

Dear Reader,

Please, don't panic! This is not the end of the story. There's one more book to go yet, and to tide you over until then, Chapter 1 immediately follows my usual message.

If you have read my other work, or if you are familiar with my story, you might know I began write this series my last year of high school. It would take several rewrites and many drafts to become what I wanted, but eventually, *Slumbering* was born in its current form, and the rest have followed faithfully.

This book is part of that original pain. I didn't have a completely happy ending to high school. I was done, but the triumph I expected was more like a tepid pleasure, which almost makes it worse than outright disappointment. Not because I didn't finish well (I did), but because so much seemed unsettled. I expected things to be finished, but they were far from over. This realization was not only unexpected, but disappointing and depressing.

I've come to see that, while time does not heal all, it does provide important perspective. Years later, as I write this, some months before my ten-year high school reunion, I can see that. It is not only my pain I understand better, but God's hand through it all. I can look back, and I can see more glory and more grace than I could see while I was facing the fire. It is indeed an ongoing, eternal moment that continues to astound me.

In the believer's journey, we go through trials and pain. Suffering is a given in this life. As my favorite line from *Cry, the Beloved Country*, says, "For our Lord suffered."

As dark and deep suffering is, love still lights the way. Love carries us through it, love lifts us up out of it, and love is waiting for us, surrounding us beyond the pain.

For this reason, part of this book's theme is courage. Be courageous. Dare to suffer for what you love, for what you believe, for what is right.

Christians are called to holiness more than happiness. There is a cost to choosing that life, to committing to that life, to continuing through to the end. It is not easy.

We must be brave. Power is at its most potent when it is laid down for love. And we know this to be true, for this is what our Lord did.

So, be brave and take heart. Hamilton and I will see you soon, next time, in the last book in this series, appropriately titled *Everlasting* (Book 7 of the Starlight Chronicles).

Until We Meet Again,

C. S. Johnson

THE STARLIGHT CHRONICLES

AUTHOR'S ACKNOWLEDGEMENTS

EDITOR

Jennifer C. Sell

Jennifer Clark Sell is a professional book editor and proofreader. She works from her home in Southern California. With her years of professional and personal experience, she offers several quality packages for authors. Find her at

https://www.facebook.com/JenniferSellEditingService.

Photo Credit: Savannah Sell

AUTHOR'S ACKNOWLEDGEMENTS

COVER ILLUSTRATOR

Amalia Chitulescu

Amalia Iuliana Chitulescu is a digital artist from Campina, Romania. Raised in a small town, this self-taught artist has a technique which is delineated by the contrast between obscurity and enlightenment, using dark elements in a dreamy world. Her areas of expertise include the use of theatrical concepts to create a macabre and surrealistic world that still maintains a highly recognizable attachment to reality. Bridging a diaphanous environment with light elements, an eerie view, she creates a dream world of dark beauty, done with a blend of photography and digital painting. Find her at https://www.facebook.com/Amalia.Chitulescu.Digital.Art

Photo Credit: Amalia Chitulescu

SAMPLE READING

Chapter 1 *from*

EVERLASTING

BOOK SEVEN of *THE STARLIGHT CHRONICLES*

C. S. Johnson

C. S. JOHNSON

THE STARLIGHT CHRONICLES

☼1☼
Beginning Again

For the fourth or fifth time in less than an hour, I looked down at my legal pad, only to realize I had no idea what was going on.

My office seemed too bright. The lights seemed too sharp. I glanced around as the client in front of me continued to babble on about some financial legal nonsense.

Everything else was in its place: My various diplomas and certificates, celebrating my undergrad and graduate degrees, hung on the wall, proudly and prominently displayed right across from the entrance; my desk was off to the side, facing the wall, with the window behind me; my books were stacked in precise order on the bookshelf, tucked in with some of my awards. Among them was my newest one, the one from the Pittsburgh Law and Order Association, declaring my position as "Best Associate Lawyer of the Year" that arrived just before Thanksgiving last month.

Outside, the streets of my adopted city were hobbled with people looking for warmth and a cozy corner to cuddle up in, all while the snow continually dumped down out of the sky.

Nothing was out of place, not even the typical, dull-looking client in front of me.

No wonder I was bored.

The room was a temple to law and intellect, and I'd made sure to erase quite a bit of my heart in the process of setting it up.

No wonder that, instead of taking notes, I'd been doodling.

Despite the fact I had suddenly caught myself not paying attention to my meeting (again), I smiled thoughtfully, almost longingly. *Raiya used to do this same thing in Martha's class,* I recalled.

Instantly, as though I'd touched some mental flame inside of my mind, I flinched. *Where in the world did that thought come from?*

I didn't like to think of her anymore. Not if I could help it.

Of course, now that I was completely against thinking about her, my mind wasn't listening to me, and I wasn't sure I could help it.

I didn't have to glance at the calendar on the wall of my office to know more than seven years had passed since that day.

Seven years. *Seven years.*

Seven years, and I still crumbled as I remembered Raiya's body as it collapsed against mine, still sucked in my breath as the last breath of her words passed me by, still felt the dying chill of the fire-feather she'd tucked into her hair as it flicked into darkness.

Seven years, and it was still much too painful for me to acknowledge that the only person I'd ever loved more than myself, I was unable to save.

"Sir?"

I nearly jumped out of my seat as I realized that I was still in the middle of a legal hearing. "Yes?" I straightened up in my seat, trying to look nonchalant, and, as was my usual, managed to succeed enough to get out of any possible trouble.

"Are you all right? You look … troubled," my client, Mr. Brown, muttered reproachfully.

I put on my most winning smile. "I'm perfectly fine, Mr. Brown. I am just making some extensive notes on your business concerns so we will be ready with the rebuttal at the end of the trial." I tucked the drawing up against my chest, making sure he couldn't see it, just to be on the safe side.

Mr. Brown visibly relaxed. "Oh … well, good." He nodded. "For a moment there, I could've sworn you started daydreaming."

I almost shouted, *"Lawyers don't daydream!"* It took a surprising amount of self-control not to.

Instead, I laughed cordially. "No, no, sir, not at all. I assure you, I am the most capable lawyer available for handling your case. I know what is needed to get the job done."

"See to it, then," Mr. Brown said as he looked at his watch. "Well, I best be off for now. I'm to meet my wife for dinner."

"Well, don't keep her waiting on my account." I smiled. "I'll get your files pulled and we'll be ready for court as soon as the judges assign a day for it."

"Good to hear."

"Thank you for your time. Don't worry about anything. I'll have your case wrapped up in as little time as possible."

"I'll send you your retainer check in the mail." He grinned. "With a nice Christmas bonus, just to make sure you know how I appreciate your dedication."

And then Mr. Brown picked up his hat, put on his jacket, and walked out the door.

When he was gone, I just rolled my eyes. I hated representing people who weren't concerned so much with justice as with getting out of justice, but I had to do my job. I supposed.

I didn't like to think about that too much either.

When I did allow myself those small moments of reflection, I longed for another life. But I could hear a certain annoying voice in my head, chiding me for making life one big to-do list.

Then I quickly squelched my desire. I would, to this day, never admit to Elysian, my old "pet" dragon from years ago, was right. Not if I could avoid it.

I began to pack up my stuff for the day. I had my own dinner plans for tonight.

One of my best friends from my hometown of Apollo City was coming in to see me, and I wanted to have some time to prepare for the unpleasant lecture I was sure to receive.

My eyes fell to the notepad drawings I'd created while Mr. Brown was droning on and on about the unfairness of his situation, the integrity of his investment portfolio, and how his company was no doubt infiltrated with spies who had set him up to look like an embezzler.

My face softened for a moment, as the picture staring back at me was of a lovely young woman with wings fluttering out of her head. Even though the picture was not in color, I knew her eyes were the shade of the most vibrant spring violets, and her hair was the color of Christmas gingerbread. And even though the picture was not supposed to be real, the watchfulness and steadfastness of her eyes were more than mere reflections.

I sat down in my chair and looked at the picture glumly. *When did I get so good at drawing?* I wondered to myself.

I'd been only working as a lawyer here at Pharris & Dahlonega for … was it a year, already? Surely, I hadn't been doodling for all that time.

And when did I start allowing myself to think of Raiya again?

Of course, it's entirely possible I never really forgot her, I mused, *since she was the—No! I'm not going to think about it!*

I silently chastised myself as I packed up my things. Thinking about her only made it worse, I knew.

I barely remembered graduating from high school at all. When I looked back at my pictures from that time, I could tell part of me was not there.

I didn't have any pictures from the summer after I graduated. All I could remember was looking for her and not finding her, and having to drag around this emptiness in my chest all the time.

Thankfully, I'd transferred out of Apollo City College's dual enrollment program, and actual college began soon enough. I'd whisked myself away to Pittsburgh, to a new city, to a new home, a new school, and new distractions.

But no new self to go along with it. I was still in love with a memory.

Anger and sadness pushed through me; I shoved the doodles into my briefcase and slammed it shut. *I'll deal with those later. I can't think of this now. I have stuff to do …*

Once more, all of my secret longing, all of my hurt and anger, all of it was swept away under the carpet of scheduling.

"So, you're a bonafide Steelers' fan now, huh, Dinger? That's great." The man sitting across the table from me laughed heartily.

I smiled at him; he was one of my oldest friends, Mikey Salyards. "Come on, why wouldn't I? They are among the best teams in history."

Mikey stopped laughing and turned more somber. "You've changed a lot, I guess."

"I haven't changed, Mikey. I'm still the best of best of best."

If anything, I thought, *it's Mikey who's changed since high school.* The awkward teenage years and the pressure of always being in my shadow had dispersed to reveal a strong, confident, and capable (looking) person underneath. It was almost a shock for me to see my old friend looking so different.

The weird-looking beard didn't help, I silently decided. It reminded me too much of his father, and Dante Salyards was a man I was more than happy to forget.

Mikey cocked an eyebrow at me. "Maybe in your field of law," he said. "But you couldn't hold a candle to me when it comes to coaching or gym class."

"I could probably handle the PE, but I doubt I would handle the sixty-some immature teenagers running around a gym after snorting sugar," I conceded after careful thinking.

"Aw, it's not that bad," Mikey said. "There're only about forty-five students. Apollo's a pretty small district, actually."

We began laughing as our dinners came.

"Thanks for treating me, Dinger," Mikey said, cutting up the medium-rare, freshly harvested, lightly seasoned teriyaki steak before him.

"No problem. I suppose it's worth it if you're going to travel six or seven hours in the car to come and see me."

"You know," Mikey said in a careful tone, "you could make the trip shorter for me if you wanted."

I flinched. I should've known that was coming.

I side-stepped the subject. "How does Gwen feel about you coming all this way out here?"

Mikey caught on pretty quick and grinned; I was still as hardheaded as always, and he knew it. "She's fine with it. I think she'd come herself if she wasn't so worried you'd throw her out or something."

"I wouldn't do that to Gwen," I said with a huff. Goodness knows I had more reasons to hate Mikey than Gwen, and I had agreed to meet with him.

"Well, she'd probably feel more than a little awkward with the whole high school thing, too," Mikey admitted. "She is doing well though."

"Really? How nice."

Mikey frowned at my tone. "I know you're still sore at her for what happened to you, but you can't keep this up, Dinger."

"She attempted to blackmail me, before she tried to stop me from … " I shook my head, but my fists clenched. "And she blamed me for getting attacked."

"She was confused at the time."

"Please. Don't give her an excuse."

"Get over it. You didn't even love her. You were just mad she got in the way. And besides, you had—"

"Shut up. I don't want to talk about it."

"You had Raiya—"

"I told you, I didn't want to talk about it!" I slammed my fists down on the table, hard.

So much for self-control.

Mikey frowned. "Come on, Dinger! It's been years! You *still* can't talk about it?"

I gritted my teeth together. "I *don't want* to talk about it. And frankly, you're a gym teacher, not a therapist. If I wanted to talk about it, I would hire one of those to sit around and question me."

"Hey, I'm a coach, and I have to deal with my students' problems all the time," Mikey said. "I'm good at handling problems. And besides that, you should talk about it with someone. There might be a clue in your information."

I froze. "What do you mean?"

Mikey smiled; he seemed to be glad he'd finally arrived at the point he'd wanted to bring up all evening. He leaned closer and said, "Weird stuff's happening again."

"What do you mean, 'weird stuff,' Mike?" I asked carefully.

Did I really want to know? I didn't think I did. The last time "something weird" had happened, I needed to transform into Wingdinger—oh, God, how I cringed at the very thought of that stupid name—and had to save the world.

Mikey sighed. "Dad's back in Apollo City. I heard from Jason he came by, and he was asking for me. And you."

I said nothing, only remained motionless. Mikey's dad was not really a pleasant memory to either of us. If he was back in town, something was certainly up. And it certainly was going to be unpleasant.

After all, Dante Salyards was not a man who would take anything like supernatural trouble lightly. During his last stay in Apollo City, I knew Mikey's dad had seen a good extent of what trouble the supernatural could do.

But still, that selfish, peace-seeking center inside of me wanted this to be fake. So I showed no emotion or reaction as I asked, "What does he want?"

"I don't know what he wants," Mikey admitted with a shrug. "But if he's looking for both of us, I'm pretty sure it's not to give us an award or any money. Trouble's coming."

"How would you know for sure?"

Mikey frowned. "Come on, Dinger, don't get like that. We have to do something."

"You mean *I* have to do something, don't you?" I snorted into my drink.

"Well … yeah. I came all the way out here to see you and talk about it."

"I can't just get up and leave, Mikey," I told him. "I have a job. I've been working with the firm for a while now, and if I needed to take time off, I would've had to put it in months ago."

"Can't you take a leave of absence?"

"I can't just go, I just told you."

"You have to!"

"Why? Why should I?"

"For Raiya."

"Shut up!" I reached across the table and grabbed a hold of Mikey's shirt. Death was staring through my eyes as I growled, "Don't mention her to me. She's dead."

"Are you sure?" Mikey asked. We'd caught the attention of quite a few people by this time.

"What? What do you mean, 'Are you sure?!'" I nearly shouted. "I was holding her as she died!" I cringed as I looked down at my hands; they tingled at the memory of Raiya as she shuddered and breathed her last breath, her blood mingling with my tears … I felt shame-faced as I recalled asking her—begging her—to come back, to stay alive, to stay with me … and how, all of a sudden, she was gone. We were gone.

"But … she wasn't human, remember?" Mikey whispered uneasily as he glanced around to see that some of the people nearby were still looking at us. "Maybe she didn't die, maybe she just … went somewhere else."

Why had I never thought of that?

I was taken aback. Was it possible? Was it true?

Maybe Raiya hadn't died. It was possible—after all, I believed more unbelievable things; I'd *seen* more unbelievable things.

But I shook my head as the last remnants of my daydreams melted away in the cold light of reality. "It doesn't matter. If she wasn't dead," I said slowly, "she would have come back to me."

I might have believed it, but I still felt dumb for saying it.

"Maybe she's trying, and you're just not there." Mikey raised his eyebrows, no doubt silently congratulating himself on his advanced logic.

It was enough to get me to release him.

I allowed Mikey's remark to settle in my mind. It didn't make any sense. Why would she come back now? What else was going on? I wondered this and questioned Mikey on it.

THE STARLIGHT CHRONICLES

Mikey took a bite of his steak and said, "Like I said, there's a bunch of unexplained events going on … and Dante promises it's not even half of it. I can't explain it, but you're not there and Raiya's not there—"

"You just said she wasn't dead!"

"Hey, give me a break. Rachel would be the first one to know right? And Jason hasn't said anything about her saying stuff like that."

I remembered the bright-eyed redhead who ran my favorite coffee shop when I was in high school. Years later, I still had nothing to compare to Rachel's food. Even the steaks and lobster fillets I billed to my bosses were unable to fill the longing my stomach carried since I moved.

"How is Rachel?" I asked, deciding I'd had enough of the gloomy topics.

Mikey shrugged. "She's fine. Pregnant, actually."

"Oh? Really?" Images of a recent dream popped into my head. A little girl with red hair, smiling as she chased a smaller boy with brown hair and matching violet eyes. Rachel's children? Is that whose kids those were?

It was possible, I supposed.

"It's a girl, they know that much," Mikey continued on, not realizing I was caught up in my own thoughts. "She's due in the spring; she and Lee announced it at their anniversary party this summer."

"Do you think she'd really come back?" I whispered softly.

Mikey sighed. "Let's change the subject. Here." He pulled out an envelope. "I was going to mail this, but it's okay to give it to you now."

I opened it and quickly scanned through the letter. Then I went back and read it again, properly this time, just to make sure I understood it. I groaned to myself, but put on a smile for Mike. "You and Gwen are getting married, huh?"

"Yeah." There was nothing but joy in his big, goofy grin.

So I humored him. "That's great, man."

I humored him, and he caught me. Mikey laughed. "Come on, you're going to have to do better than that."

"You can't blame me for not being excited," I snorted. "This means I'll have to go back home."

"And not to mention be my best man," Mikey added.

"Are you kidding me?" I felt oddly conflicted. Like I should agree to it, but I would rather stick needles in my eyes or puke up a pig.

"No. I'm asking you to be my best man."

"Okay, sure, I suppose." But this better not be a lot of work, I added silently.

"Great!" Mikey grinned. "Wedding's in two weeks, so I'll be looking forward to my bachelor party—"

"Two weeks? What do you mean, two weeks?" I looked down at the invitation again. Yep, two weeks. "I can't get off from work just like that."

"Ah, don't be such a sour-butt, Dinger. Everyone else is coming. Besides, you can't really like your job that much."

"Huh?"

"I saw you when you came in. You're tired and exhausted, and probably sick, too. You don't seem to care, either. I can tell. We've been friends a long time."

"That's not the truth."

"It's a good part of it."

I grumbled, caught. It had been forever since someone was so good at reading me. "That's not the whole picture."

"What else is there? Is Charlotte still giving you grief?"

I moaned at mention of her. I put my head in my hands. "You've got a point there, I suppose."

Charlotte was one of the first friends I made in college. I remembered only introducing myself to her because I'd thought, foolishly, she was actually Raiya. Charlotte had the same long, reddish-brown hair as Raiya, and looking at her from behind, I was too hopeful to be cautious.

But Charlotte had been more than gracious to me, even helping me get my current job at her father's law firm, and we were friends—but that was the problem, for her, of course.

She'd been bugging me lately with hints of how we should be dating. Or married with seventeen children and living down in the South with her mother's side of the family. I wasn't sure which she wanted, but I was terrified to discover the specifics.

"You don't have to bring her to the wedding." Mikey smirked.

"I wasn't going to. But she did get me the job at her dad's office. That's why I don't think I can just get off."

"Come on, surely he'll be okay with it."

"I'm not worried about him. It's my other boss, Pharris, who's the real piece of work."

"Piece of work" was the kindest way of putting it. How do you explain to scientists that you've found the missing link between humans and the Tyrannosaurus Rex? Everything from her meticulous, over-gelled bob to the edge of her gilded fingernails screamed dinosaur DNA. If that wasn't enough, her attitude and tone sealed the deal.

"Just ask," Mikey said. "And if you can't get off, well, just quit. You don't like it anyway."

"I'm good at it."

"So what? You need something in your life that you love."

"Look, just get off my back, will you? If a miracle happens and I can get off work, I'll do it. But short of that, you'd better call up Poncey."

Mikey grinned, and for a moment, I had to laugh; Mikey looked just like his high school self, with food stuck in his teeth, his smile wide and innocent. "If that's the best I can get from you for now, I'll take it. Besides, given our history, I'd say a miracle is right around the corner."

"Ha, ha, yeah right." I rolled my eyes. I'd forgotten how to believe in miracles.

THE STARLIGHT CHRONICLES

READY FOR BOOK 7?

Thank you for reading! Please leave a review for this book and check for other books and updates!

Thank you for reading!

Please leave a review and check out my other books

for more wonder, adventure, and fun!